The Poet & The Angel

JENNIFER CHAPIN

The Poet & The Angel
Copyright © 2019 by Jennifer Chapin

Tellwell Talent
www.tellwell.ca

ISBN
978-0-2288-1173-2 (Paperback)
978-0-2288-1174-9 (eBook)

Dear Anna...
Thank you for
buying my book
and I wish you
all warmest
wishes.
Enjoy!

Janet

Foreword

In August of 1936 Federico Garcia Lorca, Spain's Man of Letters, was executed in Granada, Spain by the fascists at the outset of the Spanish Civil War. His body was never found.

There is much speculation as to why he was murdered. Some say it was because he was gay, and in machismo Spain this would not have been tolerated.

Some say he was a "Red" and that he had entered his own war of wills against the fascists and the Catholic Church, their allies.

Whatever the reason, there is documented evidence that the fascist general who signed his death warrant said that Lorca's words were more destructive than ten thousand guns and that he needed to be silenced.

This book gives Federico Garcia Lorca back his voice, if only for a day.

For Federico

.

I have seen the blood
Of Spain rise up against you
To drown you in a single wave
Of pride and knives

Pablo Neruda

I spent the night in Aidadamar, feast-
ing in its pastures, and in its dwell-
ing places I had my fill of love.

Whenever the East Wind blows it carries me its
scent and evokes the spectre of the lost loved one.

Abu l-Qasim ibn Qutiya

Prologue

When Angelina threw open her shutters, weary and wooden with time, the first thing she saw was a skylark hovering in the mists over the Alhambra. It hung suspended on the breeze, wings outstretched. Its plaintive cry pierced her heart. She watched the bird's progression as it circled the ancient battlements slowly, as though looking for something irretrievably lost. A solitary ray of light touched its wings as the bird spun slowly into the clouds, and then, with a heartrending cry, it disappeared completely.

She had no way of knowing that what she had witnessed was an omen that would change her life. She had no indication that by the end of that day, she would have travelled to the moon and the stars, hard as ice and diamonds, and then wafted back to Earth on the sighs of a gypsy tambourine.

She could not have told you that the skylark's presence would have opened a door to her city's Arab past. She never would have dreamed that she would hear the cries of Boabdil, the last Caliph of Granada, Spain, as he surrendered his sword to Queen Isabella and King Ferdinand in 1492. These were monarchs that in history were marked for their absolute and rigid Catholicism. Nor would she have imagined the scorn of Boabdil's mother as he did so, a scorn that berated his manhood as they were driven out of Granada, like common curs.

She did not comprehend that the Catholic reign of the beloved monarchs she had been taught to revere in school had its beginnings in blood and in the laying to waste of the last vestiges of the Arab world in Spain, without mercy. Nor did she understand that these devout monarchs, with their Inquisitors in tow, had led an impassioned crusade against the Moors and the Jews, and when they were conquered, they forced them to bow to one they called "prophet" but not God. In the end, they were driven from their land and a way of life they had shared since the dawn of their collective memory, where they lived side by side, in harmony.

Angelina had not fully understood the complexity of the hatred that saw General Franco emerge as "victor" in a continuation of the earlier Catholic crusade. It was a Civil War in the 1930s that tore their country apart and left them divided and broken in spirit. Isolated from a world that turned their backs on them in their time of need, it was the poets, artists, and visionaries that fought the war against "El Caudillo," Hitler, and Mussolini. She did not comprehend that had Europe and North America come to their aid, the Second World War may have been averted, and Hitler stopped.

And Guernica too could have been spared, leaving Picasso to more tranquil meditations.

What Angelina had not learned at school by the time she was eight years old was that when the Nationalists won this battle, the people were cowed into a complicity of silence and "forgetting," leaving the ghosts of their ancestors to writhe in the ditches of unmarked graves. And their bodies lay there still, paved over by a Faustian modernity.

After all, she was just a little girl stretching up her arms to heaven, in rapture.

Chapter One

There was an early dusting of morning sun on the Alhambra now, and Angelina stood by the river Darro watching the swallows sweep over its ramparts like lovers. Round and around they swirled, as though Moorish guardians had returned once again to keep watch over her. The air whispered of jasmine.

As she ran through the narrow, cobblestone streets of the Albaycin district, swept smooth by passion and infamy, she heard the bells ring out from the church of Santa Ana, a crystal ache in the morning air. She skipped down passageways between tall pink and ochre houses, their roofs aging and musty-tiled. Bits of ancient grass sprung up here and there amongst the tiles, in defiance.

Climbing down broken steps, she passed a sculpture embedded into the wall of a church. A man embraced a huddled multitude who knelt at his feet, weeping. His eyes gazed heavenward as though he were imploring God for mercy. Grief and heartbreak drove wedges into his face, and his tears poured down like a river, sweeping across the charges in his arms.

Angelina ran past, hearing only the rumbling of early morning conversation from the shuttered spaces around her. The sounds began as a murmur and then wafted through the alleyways softly, desultory and languid, not yet strident, perhaps it was the hour. Then other voices joined in from nearby dwellings, the mews and the yawns of an early rising sweeping over her like a discordant symphony. It arose from behind lattice windows and doors, and from within hidden courtyards. Hidden, always hidden, in Granada.

As she approached Bib-Rambla Plaza in the centre of the ancient city, she could see that the farmers of the Vega were setting up their stalls in the shadows of the great cathedral; there were stacks of zucchini, potatoes, purple onions, and the ubiquitous oranges of Valencia. The vendors moved silently amongst the produce, balletic in their poise and concentration, preparing themselves for the daily onslaught.

Around the corner, the herbalists were engaged in a similar exercise. They fussed over their stands of mysterious remedies like old women gossiping at a country fair; their shadows cast into relief against the cathedral behind them, making them look like giant puppets from a world beyond. Pot after pot of herbs and spices lined the boulevard, fragrant and pungent: rosemary, coriander, lavender, garlic, and pepper. Some promised relief from hair loss to impotence, from an irritable stomach to a broken heart.

Angelina ran past them and then skipped down an alleyway to see her friend, Emanuel Borella. She waved at him through the window of his "herborista," but he didn't see her, so intense was his concentration. She tapped on the window, but his focus did not change. The soft light of morning slanted in through leaded windows, and dust motes floated around his head like cherubs in flight. He bent over his herbs muttering strange incantations like an alchemist, his hands weaving ancient spells as he did so. And so, without disturbing him, she moved silently past.

The cafés had started to open in a kind of dreamy, lemon haze. Yawning waiters stretched forward the canopies in anticipation of a hot day. Others stood by and watched them, carelessly smoking with one hand, gesticulating with the other, their voices loud against the sepulchral silence of the morning. Smoke and loud chatter, tousled hair and tired eyes, laughter and smiles as they drank their chocolate and ate their churros and looked around indifferently for customers.

Angelina sailed past them into the plaza, her

arms open wide like an airplane. She twirled round and round like a spinning top, her hair an aureole of red and gold. Her skirt swirled around her in fuchsia disarray, like the petals of a flower opening its arms to the sun on a warm summer day. She ran past the Floristerias of Carmen, Ana, Antonia, and Piquale as the owners opened their stalls to bring out white lilies, yellow carnations, and bright, red roses, releasing their perfume into the air.

Freedom!

Chapter Two

S he would have missed him completely if the sight of an old brown shoe sticking out from behind the fence of Neptune's fountain hadn't stopped her. It looked scuffed and forlorn, forgotten. Its seams were desiccated and weary, full of the dust of the road and troubled dreams. But as Angelina reached over to grab it, the shoe recoiled quickly, and she realized with shock that it was attached to a leg.

"Don't touch me! Leave me alone! Don't hurt me!" It was a voice full of panic.

The little girl jumped back and stuttered an apology. As she turned to run for her life out of the square, something stopped her. She looked back and saw through the purple bougainvillea and yellow wisteria a huddled man, weeping. He was small and delicate and had the heart-shaped face of a sprite. His skin seemed translucent, and thick black brows formed punctuation marks over dark eyes that smouldered with a gypsy's passion on a moonlit night. Angelina looked past his eyes and moved into his heart, and what she saw there frightened her. There were monsters, gnashing and desperate, grotesque in their mien. They howled around the man, lashing out at him with the agony of a thousand deaths. From their maws came a haunting, lonely sound, like wailing of wolves on a bleak night in the Vega. Great swaths of black and red swirled around them as they tormented him, without surcease. The man raised his hands to his eyes. Great hiccupping tears splashed down his face, merging with the water that cascaded down from the fountain.

But as she peered closer, she could also see a shiny golden light. It arose from the heart of this man and pushed at the edges of his grief insistently. Its presence was like a balm on a grievous wound, keeping the demons at bay.

Seeing this, Angelina was reminded of a trip that she and her family had taken to the seaside one sunlit day, before their world changed. It was a holiday away from the heat of Granada in July, a rare moment set aside for the pursuit of pure joy. She and Cristina laughed and sang and ran along the beach chasing seagulls out to sea while their Mama and Papa embraced on a blanket and watched them, laughing. Later, they scampered along the beach and stopped for lunch beside a lighthouse. The fog rolled in quickly, and what was once bright blue and golden became a thick misty grey as their world became filled with a bone-chilling cold.

The lighthouse stood firm against this intrusion, however, and pierced the fog with its bright, white light. The gloom melted in those moments and bathed them in an ethereal glow.

Angelina saw this glow around the huddled man and felt braver. She took a few steps forward, looking around to see if anyone else had noticed him, but there were few people in the square at this hour. Those that were present barely glanced in their direction, as though they did not exist. But how could they not see him, how could they not hear his cries? What should she do next? Her hands twisted nervously in the folds of her skirt.

The man turned away from her and curled himself up into a little ball against the side of the fountain. His shoulders shook silently as the water from Neptune's trident poured over him in sympathy. The sun, once radiant, disappeared behind a cloud and doves circled around him, uttering a heart-rending lament. Then suddenly, great sadness filled the square.

It began as a gentle sigh from behind the transept of the cathedral and rolled like a wave across the plaza. It paused on balconies that were festooned with bright red, blue, and yellow tapestries. It swept over the laughter of the waiters causing them to look up in alarm, and then it finally took up residence in the heart of the Madonna and Child whose sculpture lay in a niche on a wall close by. Mary looked down at the little girl with a sad and knowing smile, their eyes meeting in complicity. Angelina silently mouthed a prayer to her before looking back at the man and sinking to her knees before him.

"Señor?" she whispered.

He didn't seem to hear her.

She cleared her throat. "Señor?" she said louder, reaching over and shaking his arm gently. There was no response.

"Señor!" The shaking was more vigorous.

Slowly and with great effort the man uncurled his body and turned to face her. His glance crossed hers briefly and then he looked up into the sky as the sun, braver now, appeared once more and began to caress the tears on his face.

"Señor. Why are you sitting in the flowers? Why you are crying?"

His mouth moved silently and for a moment Angelina thought he was praying, so intense was his expression. She moved closer to hear.

His whispers were inaudible and so she said, "Señor, I can't hear you!" and moved closer still.

And then she heard his voice, as distant as the mountains on a cold, winter day, and just as bleak.

"My God, my God, where were you? Why did

you forsake me?" His hand went up to his heart as though to staunch the tide of pain that flowed out of him. And then he went silent.

"Señor?"

"Where were you when I needed you? Where were you that morning? I had to face them alone. Am I not your child? Did I not go to Mass every Sunday to be with you? Where were you when your child cried out for you? Oh my God, where were you? Why did you abandon me when I needed you the most?" His voice faltered and broke. He covered his face and started to weep once more. The sun disappeared again, leaving them shivering in the shadows.

Angelina twisted her hands together and looked up to the Madonna for support. Then she shook his shoulder again.

"Señor?" Her voice pleaded with him to notice her.

With great effort, as though returning from a faraway land, he looked over at her. Then he wiped his eyes with the back of his hands. He started to speak but with great difficulty, as though he were a mendicant that had come from a faraway land and been forced to pick up the threads of language once more. His voice moved barely beyond a whisper, and his hands started to move with increasing agitation.

"They left me! They left me!" He paused as the

immensity of his sadness swept over him and he wept once more.

"Why did they leave me?" he continued. "They were my friends, those I had known since we were children playing in Fuente Vaqueros, my childhood village. How could they have done this to me? Was I not their friend, their brother?" The man began to shiver and wrapped his arms around his body.

Angelina started to speak but he held up his hand to stop her. "My friends abandoned me. I did not see them when I was in prison. I did not see my own family, well except for my nanny who bought me food, pens, and the bounty of her solace and love. Where was my family? Why did they not come to see me, how could they not save me? Were they ashamed of me? Were they afraid of what might happen to them if they visited me? I was stupefied, I was in shock, and though the guards did not see, I cried. I cried every night. Oh, not at first; I thought it must be a mistake, my arrest. Wasn't I at the home of a great friend when they came for me? Weren't we playing Chopin on the piano as a duet and eating those little cakes that his mother used to make, cream and puffed pastries, the ones I loved the most? Weren't we regaling ourselves with laughter and poetry? He was a poet too! Weren't we constructing an impromptu play about the regime and the pantomime of justice that was Spain? Both of us, and my great friend was a Falange leader! I thought I was safe with him.

"Oh yes, my friends told me to flee. 'Flee! this regime hates you, they will kill you!' But I wanted to stay with my family and my friends." He paused, holding his breath.

"The same family and friends that I did not see when I was in jail. Oh yes, I saw the soldiers! Do you know that I was thought to be such a great enemy of Spain that they had soldiers with guns on the street in front of my friend's house, and on the rooftops too? In fact, the whole street was filled with soldiers! They were all very serious and had their guns trained on me. On no one else but me. I started to laugh and thought, 'This would make a great play!' but then I saw that their actions and their hatred were real, and not a play at all. And so, I got very afraid."

The man grew silent and looked over her shoulder, his eyes far away. Angelina, whose sensitive heart always picked up on another's pain, started to feel his sadness move into her heart. She gripped her hands together tightly.

"Did they even try to save me? Why was I left to be killed like a dog on the street? Why was I left to face my executioners alone? Why did I die without seeing the faces of those I loved?"

He started to cry again and dropped his head

into his arms, pulling up his knees to his chest and hugging them tightly. Angelina didn't know what to do. She thought and thought, her face frowning in concentration. She was always good at making people laugh; she was always good at stopping people's tears. This was her role in her family: she was a little jester, and it always seemed to work. But this was different. This was a pain that she had never seen before. Oh yes, she felt this pain within herself a lot, especially after the tragedy. But she had never seen this kind of pain in another. This was a newer pain, deeper somehow. Maybe she should call someone for help. But who, and where would she start? Where were his family and his friends? How could they have left him alone like this? She edged closer and thought about what she should do.

Then she remembered a lullaby that her Mama used to sing to her and Cristina when they were little. It always worked when they couldn't sleep or woke up from a bad dream of wolves in the forest or ogres with big sticks crawling through their windows. This might work. So, she climbed over the fence and sat down beside him. She pulled up her knees and hugged them too. Then she started to sing, her high sweet voice ringing out like silver.

She sang of beautiful flowers that danced and played in her garden. She sang of trees who were so enchanted by the flowers that they joined in too.

Their joyfulness affected the cows in the field, and the sheep, and even the dogs that were trying to corral the sheep. Before you knew it, flowers, trees, cows, sheep, and children were dancing a merry jig around the field, and then the clouds joined in. Angelina started to clap and giggle as she sang. Her voice wafted over the top of the fountain and kissed Neptune's cheek before it soared around the cathedral and disappeared into the heavens.

The man stirred a little and then his tears subsided. Slowly, he raised his head to look over at her. He saw her dimpled smile and bright happy eyes, and his tears stopped completely.

She finished her song and then sat quietly beside him.

"Little one, you must be an apparition; are you from heaven? Thank you for your song." Angelina smiled at him.

Then he said slowly and with great effort, "But don't you see? I was happy like you once too. This was my Granada, this was my home, and I was their favoured son. I laughed and played in the streets of this town and in the Vega beyond for as long as I can remember. I was loved by them then. As I grew, they listened to my poems and applauded my plays. They were proud of me once! But when it became expedient to do so, when the cords of oppression tightened, and they made the decision to save their own lives at the expense of their souls, the townspeople betrayed me. In the heat of that August morning when I was left standing amongst the scrub and the olive trees facing my executioners, they slept, safe in their beds; I stood high in the hills overlooking my city, crying out to a god I no longer believed in, crying out to my family and my dearest ones, but only the echo of the mountains came back to me. They left me to die alone! No one I loved was with me when the firing squad pulled the trigger. No one was there to feel my pain.

"I was in shock: 'Wait! There must be some mistake! I am only a dreamer of dreams and a lover of life. Why are you killing me? For my love of justice, for my love for the kind of people you despise, like the gypsies? For my love of freedom?'" His voice shook, and he sat quietly for a moment.

"'Or is it that you hate me for my disgust at the hypocrisy of those who govern, and their minions, the Catholic Church and the Guardia Civil? Tell me, is this why I must die?'"

The man's lower lip started to quiver as he ran his hands through his hair with rapid, agitated movements.

"And I knew them, little one; that was the worst thing of all. I knew the men who fired the guns. They were entertained and greatly beloved by my family. We would spend our days together when we were young, wild and free, tormenting our mothers as little boys do, while they chased after us, scolding and laughing. We grew up together; we dreamed together; we created new worlds and fought dragons and knights together like Don Quixote did, each of us seeking our next great quest. And so, when I looked into their eyes at that moment, at the moment of my death, my own eyes beseeched them, but they would not look at me, they would not lift their gaze from the trigger, so great was their shame. And I knew then, this was my last fleeting thought, that our friendship had been a fraud, a chimera, and that they, like Judas, had betrayed me."

He grew silent once more.

Angelina, worried that he was going to start crying again, said quickly, "But, Señor, do you think that this was bad dream? Maybe you had a nightmare about these men and what they did to you. Would that be possible? I think that might be possible."

She sat and chewed her lip for a moment and wondered how she was going to tell him. The she took a deep breath.

"I can see you, Señor. I can hear you cry and watch your tears fall from your eyes. Would I be able to see you, Señor, if you were dead?"

The man looked over at her more intensely and wiped his eyes on his sleeve. It was then that she noticed little brown holes all over his shirtfront and neck, as though a moth had eaten its way through his clothes and skin. The little holes were the colour of rust.

"But that is not possible, little one. How can you see me? How can you see me, when I am a ghost?"

"I don't know, Señor, but I can. I can see you as well as I can see anyone. But then my Mama says I see a lot of things that others don't see. She thinks that maybe I make all of this up, but that's not true. I don't make anything up; it's all real to me. So, when I read my storybooks, they always come alive with the little creatures I read about. They sit beside me and watch me read and then the little elves and fairies dance and play with me afterwards." She shrugged. "This is normal for me.

"My Mama also tells me I dream too much, and she is always trying to make me grow up and become sad like her. But I don't want to! I don't want to be sad like her. So, I bury my head in my books and fly away to distant lands and places filled with knights and their ladies, and sometimes I even travel to other worlds and get lost in the clouds. It's a better world that I go to. But I always come back, even though it's hard for me to sometimes."

She stopped, and her face became serious. "I believe in magic, Señor, even though I am told not to by people whose world is sad without it. Maybe that's why I can see you when others cannot."

The man reached over and touched her cheek wonderingly. "Little one, this is hard for me to understand! How can you see me when I have drifted like a wraith through this land for an eternity? When I have haunted the walls of my ancestral home endlessly? When I am tortured by memories that surface like sunlight on water, of my family moving in the mists around me, hovering over their happy child, while the scent of the river drifts in through the gauze of our doorway, infusing itself with our family's love? When I can still hear my mother singing to me, holding me tightly on her lap, the folk songs of the Vega washing over me with so much happiness? These sensations haunt and torture me. They are a dream, a dream of a perfect time I believed would always continue. And then darkness engulfed us all."

His face grew grave and then he sighed, turning to her. "How can you see me, when others cannot?"

"I don't know why the others can't see you, Señor, but you are as real to me as my own Mama. Would I be talking to you like this if I could not see you?"

They sat together in silence and watched as little rainbows appeared around the fountain, over the flowers, and then danced around them under a now confident sun.

She leaned towards him shyly, and asked, "Señor,

what is your name? Do you have a name? My name is Angelina. Can you tell me your name?"

The man looked at her sadly for such a long time that Angelina started to get worried again. Then he stirred. "My name? You want to know my name?" He looked over her shoulder and into the labyrinth that was the heart of Granada. His face became a cloud; his eyes raged thunder and the sadness of a sky that weeps without relief.

He looked back at her woefully. "I am the Poet, little one," he said softly. "That is my name."

"But, Señor, how can that be your name? That is not a name! Can you tell me your real name?"

"I am the Poet, little one," he repeated with great effort. "That *is* my name."

Chapter Three

Angelina tiptoed through the marble foyer towards the stairs. She could hear voices coming from the sitting room on the lower level. Peering through the balcony, she noticed with dismay that her Mama was entertaining Doña Tomaso García Ronaldes, the wife of Granada's mayor. It was Angelina's special mission to avoid the Señora on her many visits to their home. This was easy to do. Upon her arrival, which was accompanied by verbal gesticulations that resounded stridently through the walls of their Casa, she inevitably shuttered herself away with her Mama. Her pontification on the evil of the world, her self-righteous piety, and her certitude could still be heard, however. The Señora reminded Angelina of a cobra emerging suddenly from the dense green jungle grass, its head raised in midair for only a moment before it struck its hapless prey. When the visits were over and the Señora left, a cold mist trailed behind her, like a pestilent fog over the sea.

She particularly disliked Angelina, and always sniffed loudly in her presence while she scrutinized her with cold, imperious eyes. Of course, the feeling was entirely reciprocal. Over time Angelina came to understand that no matter how hard she tried, no matter how quietly she sat with impeccable manners over a series of tepid and agonizing teas, no matter how much she scrubbed the dirt from her knees and combed the tangles from her unruly hair, there was something about her that left the Señora in a state of virtual apoplexy.

She tiptoed quietly up the stairs.

"Angelina, is that you?" Her mother had the instincts of a cat.

"Yes, Mama," she sighed, as the weight of a stone moved into her heart.

"Well, come here, girl! Where are your manners? Come and say hello to our guest."

Angelina turned and trudged listlessly down the stairs. The room was shuttered in gloom. Deep shadows of regret permeated its walls, and in the space where the light tentatively entered, the blood red patterns from the paintings of the toreadors and the lament of their bulls cast an angry shadow upon the floor.

Doña Tomaso García Ronaldes was sitting on the sofa, erect as a grenadier. She looked over at Angelina, took in her flushed face and dishevelled hair, and sniffed loudly. Then she carefully picked up a piece of lint from the arm of the sofa and flicked it away in disdain.

She wore her customary black, the only note of gaiety coming in the form of a tentative ruffle of white lace around a high, starched collar. Her mouth, which had a natural tendency to droop perpetually into a frown and cause deep rivers of sadness to spread towards her neck, was drooping now and her ample bodice heaved with scorn. This caused the crucifix, one of the largest that Angelina had ever seen, and which lay captive against her bosom, to wag up and down in accusatory commiseration.

She had married Doñ Tomaso Albertino Ronaldes when she was past the bloom of youth and drifting into that uncertain realm of spinsterhood, just beyond her twenties. He was a short man of wide girth who many said resembled Napoleon. Of course, this was not a happy thought for many Granadinos as the barbarity of the French in the Napoleonic wars lay embedded in their ancestral memory.

The major strutted here and there throughout Granada, pompous and demanding, some might say with the air of the ridiculous about him, his voice loud against the flagstones of the squares. He had a Catalonian ancestry hidden within the murky recesses of his genes, some said, which made him an improbable leader in any Andalucían town. And she, the Señora, was someone he had met after his numerous dalliances in the taverns of Malaga, that coastal enclave of cutthroats and thieves, and the birthplace of Pablo Picasso.

The rumours said that after a particularly long bout of carousing, Señor Tomaso Albertino Ronaldes stumbled into the Church of Our Mother of Perpetual Sorrow to ask God for absolution from his sins, and to find a respite for his pounding head and taxed anatomy. It was there that he found her, devout before the altar and completely alone, a heavy lace mantilla covering her long, dark hair. The soon-to-be Doña Tomaso García Ronaldes turned and smiled at him as he swayed heavily toward the altar. He took this as a sign of God's providence and mercy and smiled back at her, this godsend. Then he picked a slightly wilted rose from a vase at the feet of the Madonna and tucked it behind her ear. She blushed and dropped her eyes in confusion, while his gaze roamed hungrily over her bosom and thighs, devouring her.

He proposed after a week of courtship and the parents of the future Doña García Tomaso Ronaldes, sensing that this proposal would be both the first and the last, leapt at the opportunity. And so, she had been shackled to him ever since, on the long road from Malaga to Granada, and during the painful nights of his unrelenting lust.

Once back in Granada, his kindness and passion evaporated, and she was relegated to a state of officiousness that pre-empted gaiety, wit, or intelligence. She was married to a man of importance, he said, so these qualities were irrelevant as she would always occupy a secondary position and walk in his shadow. Of course, Señor Tomaso Albertino Ronaldes continued his nocturnal visits to Malaga and afar, while his wife sat in the wreckage of her nuptial dreams and grew old.

The Señora sniffed once more. "Well, Angelina," she said in her high reedy voice. "Where have you been all morning? Your mother has been worried sick about you! What a good thing I came by here when I did, telling her not to worry. 'Your little Angelina is probably feeding beggars in the street, or patting those vile, stray dogs we see in our square, full of flees and mange,' I told her. 'But don't worry; she'll be along soon enough.' Well, girl, where have you been? Answer your mother!"

At that moment Angelina felt an urge to kick Doña Tomaso García Ronaldes on her shins. She imagined that this would cause her to howl with agony and fall back into the couch in unaccustomed disarray, losing whatever pre-conditioned state of habitual superiority she wore around her. The mask would slip and the truth of her roots, base and humble, would emerge. From this ungainly state, she would beg Angelina for forgiveness. Angelina would hesitate at first and fix her with a stern gaze, but then she would smile benevolently and say, 'All is forgiven, Señora, please don't worry,' and pat her on the hand condescendingly. And then pour her a cup of tea.

Instead, she decided to ignore her completely. "Actually, Mama, I was helping Señor Borales in his herborista." She crossed her fingers behind her back and prayed that God would forgive this little transgression. "He needed help mixing his herbs and I said I would be happy to assist him, and then oh my! The time had gone by so fast and so I ran back here as fast as I could. I'm sorry, Mama, if I upset you!" Her fingers were starting to cramp painfully.

"Oh, Angelina," her mother looked at her with a sigh. She too was dressed in black, having decided years ago to put aside her finery for the clothes of an ascetic.

"What am I going to do with you? You're a vagabond! You're no better than the gypsy children we see in the Sacramonte, living in their caves like wild animals. Or being carried by their mamas, heads held high, dreaming of flamenco as they wave their sprigs of rosemary in our faces and try to tell us our fortunes. *Our* fortunes! What about their own?

They should be concerned about their own miserable condition instead of casting the 'evil eye' upon us when we refuse to acknowledge them."

She shook her head and said, "We will have to start making you more civilized, Angelina. People will start to think you're a gypsy too."

Angelina wondered if her Mama had the gift of sight, because before they discovered her, she was trying to sneak into the kitchen to get the Poet some food and a flask of wine. They were planning to walk up to the Alhambra where he said he would regale her with stories about his love for the gypsies.

"I have a lot to tell you about them," he had told her, after they sat for a while in the bougainvillea and then climbed out on Angelina's gentle insistence. "I have made it my life's passion to study and learn from them. So, when we meet and sit in the shade of the cypress trees of the Alhambra, I will recite my ballads to you and we will talk about why I love them so and how I grieve to see them so terribly persecuted."

"But, Señor Poet! Mama and Papa and all their friends say that these people are dangerous and that little children must stay away from them or they will turn into jinn and take away our souls. If we wander by accident close to their houses and their caves, they say we might never come back."

The Poet sighed. "Angelina, people always fear

those they don't understand. And then that fear turns into hatred. If they fear the gypsies, perhaps they fear their own gypsy souls. Or maybe they are jealous of the freedom that this soul permits. If they fear a man or a woman whose way of life is against society in any way, and here in Granada they certainly do, they fear that inclination in their own souls too. They are threatened by this freedom, and it has ever been thus. The gypsies have been hunted and hated throughout time, and it is for this reason that I began to observe them more closely. But then, I am hated too. I was especially hated when I walked this Earth, by many, and certainly by the dictator and his minions. I am hated because I am who I am, a troubadour of the soul. I hold up a mirror to society, one that reflects the truths other people would prefer to ignore: the truths about themselves; about women in our world and how they are enslaved through lack of choice and through convention; and the truths about power, within the family, the church, and the government, and how it is frequently misused.

"I was hated because of my own inclinations too. I was hated because I dared to speak out for those who were oppressed by the tyrant and his hordes of simpletons and beasts.

"But why hate the gypsies? What is it that the people fear? Why do they hate them so ardently? Do

they fear the sound of their laughter without pur-
pose or intent, the silver wafting of their voices into
the heart of heaven? Do they hate the sound of their
music, that great lament that speaks of the 'duende,'
or the demon in their tortured souls? Do they fear
the fact that the 'Gitanos' bow to no earthly god, nor
do they recognize any authority beyond their own as
they wander from land to land obeying the dictates
of their hearts and the seasonal migrations of their
families, which are everything to them? Is this what
the people fear?

"Have people become so enslaved by convention
and custom, so mindlessly following this creed or
that, so intent upon the approval of a largely mind-
less society that they have subdued the whispers of
their hearts, where divinity lies, and where 'truth'
calls them? Have they become caricatures of this
dictator or that to the extent that they have become
dwarfs, imposters occupying their bodies without
the enlightenment of their souls, minions on the
puppet strings of their masters? Yes! This is mostly
true. But the gypsies? They refuse to surrender to a
law they do not respect and a creed that is not their
own. They refuse to bow to the falsity of convention.
Their hearts are the wild places that we too once
occupied, before we traded our souls for barrenness.
That is why they are feared most of all.

"Listen to their music! Feel their passion!

Because then you will know the heart of God that lies within them. When they suffer, so does He.

"I will tell you about their world of wonder, little angel, and why they need to be free. And together we will ride their wild, white horses across the sky and caress the face of the cold, tin moon, and by the time we come back to Earth on a trail of silver stars you will understand there is nothing to fear at all."

Angela remembered his words now as she looked over at her mother. "Mama, why do you hate the gypsies so much?"

She turned to Doña Tomaso García Ronaldes. "And you, Señora, why do you hate them? Have they hurt you? I would very much to know why you feel this way."

Before the Señora had a chance to answer, her mother intervened.

"Angelina, how can you ask such a question? They are the scourge of the earth!" her Mama cried. "Look at them, thieving and insolent, wandering freely through the streets of our city as though it belonged to them!"

The Señora opened her mouth to speak as well, and Angelina watched as her mottled indignation shook her body completely.

Angelina decided to pre-empt her. "But it does belong to them, Mama. A good friend of mine told me that they have been here since the beginning of time and that it is us who have trespassed into their world."

"Trespassed? We conquered this world, Angelina! And everyone who was here before us. Further, it was the will of God that we do so. They, along with the others that we conquered, now obey our dictates. They no longer have the luxury of following their own heathen ways. But you would never know this! The way they look at you, so arrogant in their mincing walk, their eyes travelling all over you as though you were the vermin instead of them! They should go back to where they belong."

"But that is what I am asking you. Where do they belong, Mama? That is what I don't understand. They belonged here before we came. Where do these gypsies belong now if we have taken away their homes? Maybe we are the ones who don't belong, Mama. Maybe that's what they would say, and why they look at us the way they do."

Her mother started to speak but Señora Garcia Tomaso Ronaldes interjected, "Angelina, why are you speaking this vile nonsense? Where is this imbecilic chatter coming from? How can you possibly think the way that you do?" She looked over at her friend and shook her head in amazement, her mouth pinched and small.

"These people come from the devil, Angelina," she continued. "Along with the Jews and the Moors that we had to convert when this land was won back to the bosom of the Catholic Church, and to the heart of Jesus." She clutched her crucifix and held it high like a weapon, and Angelina watched, fascinated, as its edges cut deep ridges into her hand.

"The gypsies don't belong to anyone's language or custom, Angelina, they come from the pit of hell, and that is where they truly belong. Like everyone else who flouts our conventions and turns their back on our way of life, they are a curse that needs to be removed from our presence. They are an insult to civility and refinement. Look at them flaunt their degradation before us. Brazen! Brazen hussies — depraved, wanton!"

The crucifix, temporarily released from its confinement, wagged angrily in agreement as Doña Tomaso García Ronaldes carefully wiped spittle from her lips.

"Depraved? Wanton?" Angelina looked perplexed. "But I don't understand, Señora. Their children look just like me. They laugh and play and tease. We even have the same games. So how can they come from hell? And their mamas love their children the way all mamas do. They hold them in their arms as they sing, and their songs are so beautiful! I laugh and clap to hear them when they play in the square at the Mirador San Nicholas. Everybody does! Señora, do their songs come from hell too? I don't think that's true. I feel happier after I've heard them. I clap the loudest of all!"

She turned to her mother with excitement, and said, "Mama, I have made a new friend! He is a wise Poet and he told me that the gypsies are not evil at all. He said they are the heart and soul of Andalucía and they have been here since eternity. He says that they wandered here as though pulled by a golden cord from heaven because they knew they had to keep our songs for us, so we would not forget them. They are here to remind us who we are and where we came from, and who our ancestors are. My friend said they came to us on the Wings of the Most High and were sent to remind us of how far we have fallen, and how we worship stupid things, like our minds and our houses and our money, when we should be looking up, as they do."

Her mother looked at her in horror, her hand reaching up to touch a small crucifix that lay at the base of her throat.

"Up, up?" The Señora's face became an interesting shade of purple. "Yes, they would have us look up, so they could steal from us! Up, indeed! We would grow poor while they pillaged our world. And then we would become barbarians just like them. Girl, where have you heard these notions? Who is the person that you call your 'friend?'"

"My friend is the Poet, and he tells me that he

has written many ballads about these gypsies. He says he understands why people hate them because some people have hated him too and have hurt him very badly. I think he might be a gypsy too. He looks a bit like one to me!" She giggled as she thought of him but then her smile evaporated when she saw the look on her mother's face.

"Angelina, what are you saying? You must stay away from these people; you must stay away from this poet! He will fill your head with dangerous ideas and stupid thoughts. What gets into you, child, that you befriend people like this?" The Señora choked in agreement.

Angelina looked at her mother for a long time. She saw her rigidity and felt her sadness. She looked desperately for the mother she once was and could not find her. Then she felt a great sadness too and something broke inside her, close to her heart.

"Who should be my friends then, Mama? People like the Señora who sit in the darkness like you do? People who fill their lives with pain and gossip? People who prefer the shadows, just like you? Even when there are people around them who love them so much? Should my friends be those who allow the shadows to take all their soul when the flowers are just outside their window and beg for their attention? Should my friends be those who shut away the sun even though it wants to come in? No! That's stupid! I don't want friends like that, Mama. I don't want to be like that."

She turned and moved towards the door. "Maybe you should listen to the poets too, Mama. You used to once upon a time, remember? Before *she* died. Before you took your love away from me. Before you started to blame me for her death, my sister and my closest friend. The poets are full of love, like you used to be. Maybe if you listened to the words of the poets instead of crying in this room that smells like death you would become my Mama again."

Angelina's face crumbled, and without another word she turned and ran from the room, leaving her mother's gasps behind her.

Chapter Four

It was hot, and the streets were filled with the kind of dry, desperate air that sucks all the moisture out of the lungs and leaves bystanders panting for relief. There were few people on the streets and those that were there wilted as they crept down Calle Tablas. Angelina was one of them. In the midday paralysis of heat both shopkeepers and residents had shuttered themselves indoors, gasping on their divans until the cool of evening permitted them an avenue of escape. Those who ventured out did so by clinging desperately to the shaded sides of buildings like barnacles on cool, slate grey sea rocks.

Women, young and old, sighed as though the heat were yet another affliction from the Almighty that they needed to endure. They reached into their purses for their fans: lace-tipped with pictures of cool country lanes or haciendas in soft florals for the more sedate, brilliant shades of vermillion, orange, and fuchsia for the young, or young at heart. And then, as one, like synchronized dancers that had rehearsed this role for a thousand years, they snapped them open and fanned the air around them, frantically.

Angelina walked into the hotel. The Poet wanted her to meet him here before they began their long ascent to the Alhambra. It was imperative that she do so, he said. The lobby was cool and dark, a welcome respite from the heat. The room was baroque in its furnishings, elegant and refined, with dark panelled walls. It looked as though this had once been the home of a respectable family. Antiques and wood carvings, Tiffany lamps, and beautiful, soft paintings formed its decor.

There was a picture of the Poet in an alcove at the end of the room. It was taken in June 1936, two months before he died. She went over to look. It was an elegy of some kind, a memorial, words of loss written about him over the years, gestures of shock at his tragic passing. The Poet's picture was taken in profile. It seemed to Angelina that he was offering solace to those who took his picture. There was a gentle smile on his face that embraced them.

There were few people in evidence in the hotel. A distracted waiter appeared momentarily with a tray that was precariously perched and then, without glancing in her direction, disappeared into the inner recesses of the kitchen. Angelina observed hot steam, raised voices, bickering, and then silence once more as the door swung shut behind him.

She heard him before she saw him. The sad tinkling of a piano reached her, its melody leaving her transfixed. It was both poignant and rapturous at the same time, and so heartfelt that she started to cry. The notes travelled across the Vega and through his broken dreams. They ran up and down gentle hills and wound their way through the olive groves, getting caught up in their gnarled beauty before disappearing into a cascading river, like silver tears. Angelina was immobilized by their beauty; this was a beauty that spoke of longing, a formless dream of longing and regret, as though something had been irrevocably lost. The music travelled up her spine and caused her to shiver with both sadness and wonder, as she remembered her own loss.

Then everything fell silent.

She followed the dusty echoes of the notes and found him, sitting quietly on a piano stool. His hands lightly touched the keys and he stared vacantly into space. He had changed his clothes and wore a tuxedo now, with a crisp white shirt and a black bow tie, as though he were going to a ball or a fête. Yet his feet were bare, and this, along with his tousled hair, gave him the look of a rakish street urchin. He trembled. She looked through his heart and saw him in this very room in another time. Surrounded by friends and laughter, he was the centre of great love and adulation. She sensed the poignancy in his heart now and felt his sadness.

Then she saw the words "betrayal" move through his mind. She felt his panic and sheer disbelief. These emotions moved through him like discordant notes and swept aside the melodic beauty that had preceded them. Through his eyes, she watched as his world came to a final and desperate end. She saw his horror and felt his pain as his life seeped out of him. His final thoughts were filled with a profound bafflement and a deep despair.

Then his eyes cleared as he looked up at her. "Chopin." He smiled sadly. "Did you like it?"

Chapter Five

Angelina took his hand and led him out of the hotel to the tree-banked road that led upward to the Alhambra. There was a hush around them as the world slumbered.

They passed a statue of Saint Michael at the entrance of the path. He stood tall and sombre, his sword held in front of him. In spite of this, he looked at them with compassionate eyes.

The Poet stopped and looked up at him. "Did you know that Saint Michael is the Archangel that watches over Granada? At least, that is how I depict him in one of my poems. I call him the *King of the Globes*, because that is how I see him. I love him very much. I also talk about Saint Gabriel. In my poem I refer to this great Archangel as *'the joy of my eyes'* and the *'Scion of the Giralda Tower.'* Saint Gabriel watches over Sevilla."

He paused and then ran his hands through his hair vigorously. Angelina could see sparks of fire igniting around him in a halo. She looked up at the

Archangel for an explanation, but his eyes seemed to be fastened solely on the Poet.

"Don't you think it's funny, Angelina, that in the course of our history we have hated each other so terribly because of our supposed religious differences and yet these great ones, these great messengers of God, are loved by all. They are the commonality that unites us. They hate no one.

"It is Saint Michael's strength and beauty that captures me. I called on him often when I was in jail, like Saint Joan must have done."

He shook his head sadly. "I never understood why he couldn't save me. But I could feel his presence! His gentle touch fell on my brow and his hand touched my cheek at night. I could hear him say 'there, there,' breathing peace into my terrified heart, which gave me great solace. I must believe that there was a good reason for me to die this way, and one day I will ask him. Like Saint Joan did, I am sure."

They started their ascent and Angelina looked over her shoulder at the statue once more. It seemed that the mighty Archangel looked at them both now, his eyes filled with great love and knowing.

"Yes," she said, "I love him too. I call on him all the time, especially when my heart hurts so much that I can't sleep at night. He is my hero."

As their climb continued, the silence of the trees formed a bulwark around them. So did the gentle murmur of the water as it ran downwards on either side of the road into the city.

"Why would your heart hurt so much? Why are you so sad right now, Angelina?" he asked gently. "Where has that beautiful smile gone? You have changed. What happened to you since we last saw each other?"

Angelina looked up at him briefly and then sighed. "It's my Mama," she said. "I think she hates me and blames me."

"Hates you? Blames you? How could anyone hate such a beautiful angel? They may admonish you for asking the sun to stay out a little longer from time to time or encouraging the trees to dance a little more wildly in a lightning storm upon the Vega. But surely nothing more than this! What could you have possibly done that would cause her to blame you for anything?"

Angelina was silent for a moment and then grasped his hand more tightly. She told him about Cristina. She told him about the accident and how she couldn't save her. She told him about that day on the beach when she and Cristina were digging for clams and how in the brief interval of time when Angelina rushed to the top of a cliff to look for birds' nests, a rogue wave had swept over the marshlands and washed Cristina away. She told him how much horror she felt as she reached out her hand to try and stop the wave, her parent's screams rivalling her own. She said that Cristina's death weighed on her heart completely. It pressed the life out of her sometimes, so she couldn't breathe at night. She told him how she felt her mother's sighs like daggers in her heart. She wore the dark mantle of full responsibility for her death.

Angelina told the Poet that for months after the tragedy, she writhed in agony. She felt her sister's death like an open wound that wouldn't heal. The same nightmares tormented her night after night: of reaching out across the roar of an unforgiving sea, white-crested and terrible like an avenging demon, touching Cristina's hand for a moment before she disappeared completely.

She would awake sobbing from these dreams, she told him, and then she would reach over to see if her sister was still in bed with her. When her touch yielded back only the coldness of the sheets, and when she saw the deadness of the pale pre-dawn light glaring at her, she would start to cry again. It was only with the filtering of the sun through the window slats that the terrors of the night would subside. The malevolent jinn, now satisfied with the mayhem they had provoked and the wounds they had left in her heart, would finally leave.

"It's my fault; it's my fault that she died!" she

would cry to her father when he rushed in to soothe her.

"Hush, Angelina," he would always say, "it's not your fault. It is God and not you that determines how long we live and when we must die. Do not distress yourself over this. It is not your fault. We don't understand the inscrutable will of the Almighty and why a little child must die; we will never understand this! But we must believe that she watches over us now and maybe she is the brightest star we see on the coldest night, twinkling and laughing and waving at us merrily. She is still with us, Angelina. We must believe that."

Then he would tell her about her Mama's nightmares. "You see, Angelina, it is different with your Mama because Cristina's ghost still haunts her. She creeps into the windows at night, especially when the moon is full and dances with Orion across a windswept plain. She wraps herself into your Mama's heart and weaves herself into her dreams. Then she slips away with the moon at the light of dawn, kissing your mother goodbye and leaving her desolate once more. She doesn't visit anyone else," he said.

But her mother's cold and anguished face told her that Angelina was to blame and the sadness, always present in the room like a plaintive wail, would take residence in her heart again. On the day that she lost her sister, she lost her Mama too.

She longed for the days of "before" when their lives were so happy. She remembered giggling as they lay under the covers at night, their sheets twisted into the shape of a makeshift tent, its centre held up by a broom. Angelina would tell her stories of Ali Baba and the Forty Thieves, making grotesque faces with a flashlight until Cristina screamed with terror and delight. She was her sister's doppelganger, her court jester, and her clown, and Cristina was her mirror, the other half of everything she was. She was her best friend. She fiercely protected her and dared anyone to get too close or she would beat them up. Everyone in her family adored her, this blond cherub with the dimpled smiled and turquoise eyes, slanted and mysterious, like the Orient. Even Señora Tomaso Garcia Ronaldes liked her and would trumpet all her good qualities effusively in Angelina's presence, as if to highlight the dramatic differences between them: little lady versus tomboy, impeccable versus woefully scruffy, perfect decorum versus unending iconoclast, clever versus the absolute opposite, and so on.

But she and Cristina would just sit there and roll their eyes at each other and then start to giggle, her sister sitting like a pretty princess, long hair tied back in a pink bow, knees primly together in her Sunday dress. In contrast, Angelina, hair awry, cowlick always more pronounced in the Señora's presence, would writhe on the couch, legs splayed, her Sunday dress rumpled, and stare longingly out into the garden beyond, her ears straining for the sounds of freedom.

"Señor Poet, I look for Cristina everywhere: in the marketplace, in the streets, and along the River Genil where we played. I call out her name and pray to God to let me see her just once more, but only my cries come back to me. But what I don't understand most of all is this: I believe in magic and angels and fairies in the trees and talking animals, and so if anyone could see Cristina's ghost, it would be me. I mean, Señor, I can see you! So, why can't I see Cristina, and why is she gone from me forever?" She scrunched up her face bravely but then her tears fell like a torrent and joined the flow of the river next to their feet.

"There, there," the Poet said softly as he reached over to hold her, his face filled with concern as she wept against him. A breeze arose at that moment and caused the trees to stir in sadness. The birds themselves fell silent as they listened to Angelina cry.

"Come, let us sit a little while." He led her over to a bench under an acacia tree.

"Would you mind if told you a story, little one? Maybe this will help you to understand a little better and help you to know that your Mama doesn't hate you after all." He dried the tears from her face. "Would that be alright, do you think?"

Angelina nodded solemnly.

"Good, let us begin, but first let us sit down beside our great friend here," he said, gesturing towards the tree behind them, its gnarled branches embracing them.

Once they were comfortable, he said, "Now close your eyes and let us fly into this story together."

He waited until Angelina settled down beside him, her eyes closing slowly as she dashed a final tear from her cheek.

"Good! Let us begin. Once upon a time during the reign of Caliph Harun-al Rashid, when the rest of the world was in rags and misery and Baghdad was the heart of all that was civilized and good, there lived a wealthy merchant who had two lovely daughters. We will call them Adele and Soria. Our merchant would spend lots of time away from home; he travelled across the seas, and looked for acacia wood, like our benevolent friend behind us, along with the purple dyes of the Phoenicians. Then he would travel farther afield and barter for the jewels and riches of India, its teas along with its opium, which formed a very respectable trade in those days. The little girls missed their Papa a great deal, but they had many things to keep them happy, and a loving mother who spoiled them. So, they would spend their days playing in the courtyard within their home, chasing each other around nightingale cages and pomegranate trees and bright sparkling fountains and then they would wander into the bazaars with their mother to see all the mysteries of the world gathered there.

"But they had a very great secret, and they had to be careful! Because, you see, one of the little girls was marked from birth in an important way, and her parents had to work very hard to make sure she led a normal life. Adele, you understand, was born with angel wings on her back, tiny little gossamer threads that caused her parents to fall prostrate with reverence when they saw her for the first time. But then they had to stand back up again quickly, knowing that they must protect their little treasure from the prying eyes of the world. They went to see their Imam and told him about this amazing miracle. The Imam shared this information with the sages and the Doctor of Law, who knew a lot about angels, and their ruminations led them to believe that Allah had indeed been merciful with this couple. But they warned Adele's parents that perhaps she might only be with them for a little while, and that maybe the reason for her presence in their lives was to be as a teacher of love, which, of course, is all that matters to Allah anyway.

"So, they raised her gently and hid her wings

under rich luxurious garments and as the time passed, they forgot about these warnings. Her father grew wealthier every day and travelled farther and farther afield to find even greater wealth. He felt that he could do this knowing that his little girl was healthy and safe. How could he feel otherwise? She radiated great wellness and joy. He felt that Allah was, indeed, blessing him greatly. Soon he only came to see them every third moon or so.

"When Soria was born, the two sisters became inseparable; some would call them twins despite the years between them. They loved each other a great deal, and when Soria got older, Adele trusted her with her greatest secret. She told her that sometimes at night, especially when the air was fragrant with aloes and myrrh and she could hear wolves calling to her in the distance, she would slip out of their bed and fly away. She would soar above the city gently, skimming over rooftops and minarets and peering into the windows of the little children, blowing them kisses as they slept.

"'You see, Soria,' she told her very seriously, 'this is something that I must do, because I am part angel, and angels need to use their wings. We need to rise into the sky to kiss God and His other angels when they awake. We also need to fly with the other angels into the upper reaches of heaven to do our angel work.

"'It is important that we do this, those of us angels that are here on the earth, or we will die. We need to be in both worlds. But you must keep my secret.' Soria looked at her older sister solemnly and promised to do so.

"One day, Adele and Soria had a birthday party for one of their closest friends, and happy mayhem filled the house and spilled out into the street. The little sisters were well-loved and most of the town's children were there, except for Caleb, the town bully. On this day, he watched them sullenly from across the street, his face growing darker and darker at all this happiness. Before long, he started to threaten the girls, throwing sticks and stones at them and then laughing when they started to cry. Furious, Adele marched right up to him and demanded that he leave them alone. That stopped him in his tracks! He was momentarily stunned by the little girl's boldness, but as soon as Adele turned her back, he picked up a large rock and threw it at her. The rock hit her in the spot where her left wing grew, and shattered it.

"Adele swooned from the pain and Soria ran screaming into the house for her mother. For days and weeks after that Adele was very sick and they thought she was going to die. But one thing they knew for certain was that she would never fly again.

Her left wing now lay limp and useless against her body.

"It was only when her father came home from one of his trips that Adele smiled for the first time. She laid her hand against his tear-stained cheek and said, 'There, there,' until his tears stopped. And over the next few weeks their father's laughter and his stories seemed to bring her back to life again. But Soria knew better. She would watch Adele drift away from them from time to time, her eyes fluttering to the horizon and the stars as she whispered her tears to the sky.

"Then, over time, she started to fade more quickly. It wasn't enough for her to walk on the earth; she needed the light of heaven too. She needed to fly and to be free! And so, over time, she descended once more into the beauty of her dreams where she stayed for longer and longer, until one day she didn't wake up at all.

"Soria remembers that morning. She remembers thinking that she had never seen the sky more beautiful, the twinkling stars giving way to the most glorious colours in God's palette, indigo and purple, and soft wisps of rose, streaks of gold. She remembers that just before she opened her eyes, she felt the breath of a kiss on her forehead, fingers touching her hair and the scent of an 'I love you' in her heart. She awoke to see a trail of mist leave the room and rise up to become one of the angel clouds that were already in the sky."

The Poet stopped and they both sat for a long time listening to the sighing of the trees and the sympathetic murmur of the stream.

"Did she die then, just like Cristina?" Angelina had opened her eyes and was looking at him anxiously. She sat up and started to wring her hands, but the Poet clasped his own on top of hers and calmed them.

"No, little one, she didn't die; she just returned home, like we all will. Adele was already free from the impurities of the world. She was so white and bright in her heart that there was nothing more for her to do on this Earth, except to return to the arms of a loving God and her angels. And so that is why she can't be seen on the Earth anymore. The only trace of her remains in beautiful memories and in happy thoughts, and in the occasional whisper of love in her sister's heart."

Then they sat together hand in hand and reflected.

Chapter Six

T hey walked through the filigreed lace columns of the Nazrid Palace of the Alhambra, a fairy-tale castle drawn from the annals of Scheherazade. White-boned in the sun, its columns rose gracefully into the sky as though in supplication. A hint of a breeze moved gently through its porticos, broken only by the eerie cries of the swallows.

Despite its spectral beauty, the palace left a chill inside Angelina's heart. There was something forlorn about it, something bereft about its abandonment high in the hills overlooking Granada. She shivered as she walked across its brick floors and thought she could hear a plaintive moan sweep through its halls, like a bride who had been left at the altar while her bridegroom fled. As she strained to hear, she could also sense the echo of another time. She heard the laughter of children, followed by the chiding of their mothers. She heard their sweet songs, and their clapping hands, muffled slightly by the tinkle of the fountains. She felt the bustle of life as shadows and fleeting images of light floated around her. When she strained to see them, however, they moved away from her glance, like shy children.

The weeping palace opened a wound inside her. She felt its pain mingle with her own. It took up residence there as a beautiful woman with wild, raven hair who reached out to her in anguish, on her knees and tearing at her clothes in agony. The little girl stopped in the middle of the hall so that she could listen and try to understand her pain, but that eluded her too.

The sun slanted in through a portico and created an aureole of light around her. It played with her auburn curls and then brushed her cheek gently, while all around her the air whispered of its Arabian past. The eight-pointed star in the ceiling, rich and multifaceted; the tiled niches, in reds, blues, and bright yellows; the carved wooden archways; and the arabesques all breathed as one, in perfect synchronicity and grace. There was a faint smell of musk and cinnabar in the air, and its gentle wafting across the room caused Angelina to close her eyes for a moment and travel into the very heart of Arabia. She saw movement in the sand, warriors, fierce and uncompromising, sweeping through the desert in search of other lands. Their scimitars and turbans flashed in the sun as men and horses moved swiftly as one, clouds of dust obscuring their intensity as

they moved relentlessly forward. Following them
were their wives, children, and slaves, and their possessions. There were no hindrances to stop them
in this, their holy mission. Piety was the fuel that
drove them. That, and their love for Allah and the
Prophet. They needed little else.

The Poet's voice shook Angelina out of her rev-
erie. On the far side of the room, while running his
hand along the wall, he had stopped over an inscrip-
tion to Allah.

"Look at our history, Angelina," he said as she
approached. "Yes, 'our' history. If every mosaic and
stone could tell you their story there would not be
enough pages in the world to encompass them. We
would have to add a new *Arabian Nights* to the world
of literature. The world that the Arabs left us was
rich in beauty and meaning and, as oblique as they
were at times in their poetry, their words were filled
with the scent of a rare perfume. Their civilization
was exquisite, and it cascades towards us across time
to find its way into our hearts. We are the descen-
dants of genius, Angelina! The world of Andalucía
that we inherited was unmatched anywhere else at
that time. Scholars and poets from Asia, Damascus,
and Europe flocked here to sit at the feet of the great
ones. At a time when the people of Europe lived
wretchedly, barely out of their caves, their intellec-
tuals and nobility came here to learn from scholars

like Maimonides and Averroes; they came to sit at the feet of the poets, astronomers, architects, philosophers, and mathematicians that resided here. This was a golden age of tolerance, and it was this great civilization, this Al-Andalus, that led Europe out of ignorance and paved the way for the Renaissance. The world that was here was a bright light shining in a dark universe, and Arabs, Jews, and Christians alike all contributed to its greatness. This golden age of Arab rule, as fractious as it was at times, as internally divisive as it became, spanned close to eight hundred years, and it was the 'taifa' kingdom of Granada that was the last stronghold. This beautiful palace that we see around us, the marvellous echoes of the ancient Arab quarter in the Albaycin with their vibrant souks, was built during a time that we know as the 'Re-Conquista,' when Christendom crept slowly and painfully through Spain to reclaim her for their god. Now we 'celebrate' this ridiculous holiday every year, as though the decimation of a superior culture had been a glory for Spain instead of one of its greatest calamities, one from which it took hundreds of years to recover. But at the time, the Nazrid Caliphs, seemingly in defiance of the inevitable, built the marvel that we now see around us, and this great kingdom, this pearl of Granada, lasted until 1492. In fact, little angel, it was in this very room that a weeping Boabdil, the last Caliph, handed over the keys of his city to Queen Isabella and King Ferdinand, and Arab rule came to an end."

Angelina thought back to the sadness she felt earlier.

"But if we listen to these stones," he continued, "we can still feel their power move us. Listen to these walls, Angelina; they will tell you everything you need to know about the wisdom of our ancestors."

They were silent as they looked around the room together, and then the little girl asked, "But, Señor Poet, if what you say is true and this Arab world was so enlightened and wise, then why did the church think they were evil? Why did the king and queen destroy this civilization and the faith of the ones who ruled here? The Christians and the Jews weren't destroyed by the Arabs, you said, nor was their faith. I have heard that their churches and synagogues survived, and the people continued to pray there. So, why was this crusade carried out against the Arabs? Why did the Christians want to destroy them?"

The Poet sighed deeply. "Angelina, I reflect on these questions constantly. We must ask ourselves: was the culture that replaced what lay here before superior, or was its cruelty and intolerance towards the Arabs and the Jews a mark of its inferiority? Is God so divided against Himself that he needs great religions to hate each other so deeply and to war against one another in perpetuity? Are we not all bowing to the same God? And if it is a God that hates so deeply, then why would you want to bow to Him at all? I don't, not anymore, especially when I have seen what this 'God' has done to my country, to my family, and to me."

The Poet was silent as he looked over Angelina's shoulder and into the hills beyond the city. His gaze passed through the mists that hung over ancient battlements. His eyes wandered past the crumbling walls that marked the old city, and then, as Angelina watched, they disappeared into the heart of desolation itself.

Chapter Seven

Angelina searched his face anxiously. She was frightened by the labyrinth of fears that dominated him, and by the dark tunnel that pulled him away without warning. And as much as she tried to keep him with her, his heart, broken and sad, always seemed to want to leave again, and she knew she couldn't follow him into this dark world. This time, he seemed to stop breathing and his face took on a waxy sheen. Angelina thought she had lost him forever and reached out to tug on his arm urgently, but there was no response. He was cold to the touch and immobile.

"Señor Poet, come back to me, please don't leave me, please come back!" She started to cry and shook his shoulder harder. An eternity passed and then he finally shifted his position and turned to look at her. His gaze was foggy. It was as though he didn't remember her and seemed surprised to see her standing there. But when his eyes cleared and he saw her worried face, he smiled gently, and reached over to wipe away her tears.

"Where do you go when you leave me like this? Why do you leave me? It scares me when you do this because I'm afraid I won't be able to bring you back! And then what am I going to do? Who is going to be my best friend if you go? You will leave me, and I will never see you again! I've already lost Cristina; please don't tell me I will lose you too!" Her voice shook as she reached out and grabbed his hand and held on tightly.

"My beloved angel, you will never be alone! No matter where I am, no matter where I go, no matter if you can't see me all the time, I will always be with you to make sure you are safe; I promise! I will wrestle with God Himself just to make sure I can be one of your angels too. You are in my heart now, right here, and your kindness and friendship mean everything to me. Your love is an oasis in a barren and lonely world. I will never let you go. I promise."

He smiled and touched her cheek. "Your tears remind me of my little sister whom I love so much. When she cried because the sun had gone out of her world, I would pull her into my lap and say 'There, there,' until she smiled once more and then the sun would come out in my world again too." He dried the remaining tears on her cheeks and then his face grew serious.

"Angelina, you must understand I need to face these demons alone; I can't take you with me on this journey. Please do not be afraid for me. I know it's hard, but you must try. There is no language in the world that can convey to you the depths of my sorrow. It is like a painting by Bosch: contorted figures, grotesque, full of pain and unresolved regret. It is like a wound that doesn't heal. I feel like Sisyphus pushing that great stone up the mountain. Just when I've almost reached the top and say, 'Ah hah!' the stone rolls back down to the bottom and I wearily descend to shoulder my burden once more. I wonder in moments like this whether I will ever reach the top at all, or perhaps this is my punishment from God for some great crime and I am doomed to this cycle of endless torment. But for the life of me, I can't understand what crime I committed that would have been that severe." The Poet looked at her forlornly and started to rub his eyes.

Angelina shook her head furiously in disagreement and pulled his hands towards her.

"No, Señor Poet! You could never have committed a crime like this. Your heart is pure and beautiful. I see you! You are filled with love. What happened to you was not your sin; it was theirs. It was their sin, their evil. It was evil in the hearts of those men that caused them to do this terrible thing to you. They hated you for no reason. I don't know why the world wants to hurt people who are beautiful, people who have a kind heart, but it's true. I'm only eight years old but I have already seen this in my world. And you try to stop their hatred and their sadness, but you can't seem to stop it. It's like a huge snowball that tumbles down from the top of that mountain and gets faster and faster, taking on more and more anger, like the anger of others who join it too, until no one can stop it. And you are helpless if you try. Maybe there's a beast inside all of us. For some people, this beast makes them want to destroy beautiful things and beautiful people. Maybe it's a jealous and raging beast. I will never understand this, Señor Poet. But you must never believe that you are being punished for something terrible that you did. You did nothing wrong. They did."

Chapter Eight

He looked at her tenderly as tears rushed into his eyes and then he leaned down and kissed her cheek. "Come, beloved angel, let us put these thoughts behind us for now and walk through the gardens. Then, as I promised, I will regale you with stories about the Arab world and its wonders. I will try not to disappear again, but if I do then you have my full permission to pull me back and admonish me, without mercy!"

He held out his hand and they moved without speaking into the Generalife, the garden paradise built by the Caliphs as a sanctuary and a means of escaping from everyday life. Beyond this once lay a city of workers and artisans, two thousand strong, who laboured to keep the Alhambra flowing with precious goods: silks from Samarkand and India; fine spices of cloves, aloes, and cinnabar from Arabia; and precious tapestries from Persia. They also built the aqueducts that fed the city's soul and brought precious water down from the Sierras.

Their way of life was self-contained and flowed with a delicate balance and rhythm. It was an oasis in a parched world, as the summer months would see the perimeter dry and dusty brown whilst within the gates of the Alhambra flowers bloomed and exotic plants were lovingly tended by gardeners who, like alchemists, brought out their full palate of wonder.

The Generalife, this "heaven on earth," however, belonged to the Caliph alone. It was a labyrinth of trees and curved archways that provided solace from the mercurial heat and sheltered him, as a lover would. The gardens breathed reverence for nature. It was a place for the Caliph to contemplate the beauty of Allah's world, and to listen to music — the music of the birds; the music of water in the fountains, so precious to these former desert dwellers; the music of the flutes and of maidens singing; and the music of poetry. They were all there for his pleasure. It was in this paradise that he could truly be at one with the Divine and leave the temporal world behind.

Granada lay below, and the Sierra Mountains rose behind, white-capped and majestic in the heat of the day. The air sang of oleander and jasmine, and bright purple morning glory clung to ancient stone walls. Pomegranate and cypress trees intertwined with lilies and roses along the path. It was as if God had paused in the act of creation to love this place more than all the others and, with a delicate brush drawn from the haze of a celestial palate, had artfully touched the pathways and the flowers with gentleness, freeing every colour in wonderful exuberance. The valleys, the mountains, the hidden recesses of stone, and the hillsides all glowed with oranges, reds, and royal purple while around them, fountains of water splashed joyfully.

They stopped in the shade of an olive tree and spread a blanket of many colours beneath them. Then they sat and unpacked the bread, wine, and cheese from Angelina's basket.

"Look at the beauty of our world, little one, look at our Granada. She is my home." He stopped for a moment and then sighed heavily as he ran his hand through his black and unruly hair. "Well, she *was* my home. At one time, she was also my sanctuary and my life. Everyone I loved and cared for lived here and this is why I returned to her from Madrid at a time of great peril. My friends told me that this regime believed I was a 'Red' and had incited the people against them. 'They will do anything they can to stop you,' they said. And I said to them, 'But, surely, you must be mistaken! That could never happen. Why should I flee? I am not a *Red*; I am not political! I care for the people alone; does that make me a *Red*? I care that they are being oppressed by tyrants, by the aristocrats and landowners, by the government, and yes, even by the church. But, do I not also spend as much time with the Falange leader who loves my poetry? Do we not dine together, and do I not regale him with my latest work? I am apolitical! Besides, I need my family now, I need my friends. Look at what is happening on the streets of Madrid: people are dying! I need the comfort and refuge of my home. It is my sanity. Hasn't Granada always been my shelter and my salvation? Hasn't she always nurtured and protected me? Isn't this where, in the sanctity of my room overlooking the gardens of Huerte San Vincente and protected by the Virgin, I have written my best work? Where I played the piano for my mother and her friends? If there is trouble and strife, isn't Granada the one I always return to? She is like my mother, and I have always felt safe in her womb.'

"I said to them, 'Why shouldn't I return to her now when madness is descending upon our world? When life is losing its cogency? When our towns and villages are becoming rife with hatred, and when absurdity is becoming the norm? When ancient wounds, long festering, are starting to explode? When Spain is starting to turn against herself once more, like Medea who kills her own children?' And so, believing this, I turned my back on their pleas, and took the long train ride home.

"The memories of that trip are etched into my soul. I remember the plains and hills, brown with the heat of summer, parched and aching for solace. The only relief in this aridity, other than the olive groves, were bright red poppies that peppered the earth like drops of blood. They seemed to wave tremulously at me as I passed, their colour bleeding into the clay with a plaintive cry. I remember thinking that there was a sadness in their frailty and in the way they sought to bloom so brilliantly and briefly, in defiance of their circumstances.

"But Angelina, in all my life, I could never have imagined that when I returned, this would also be the place that would murder me."

Chapter Nine

He grew silent and looked away from her. Angelina took his hand, knowing that if she did not do so, she would lose him again. She would do everything she could to keep his attention. She said quickly, "Señor Poet, you promised me that we would talk about the ancient ones who lived here. Tell me, what was their world like? Tell me the fables! Tell me about their magic! Did viziers and sultans really walk with genies in this land? Was Aladdin here with his magic lamp? Are gold and jewels and knights and their steeds frozen in time in caverns under our feet, waiting for someone to break an evil spell? Was the world full of poetry and magic and beautiful fairy queens that granted wishes? I want to know all that you know!"

He laughed and ruffled her hair. "All right, little angel let us talk of this world. But first, I want you to close your eyes and dream. Dream of all the magical places that you've ever wanted to visit. Let us get on that magic carpet and travel to them right now.

Think of the exotic places of wizards and talking trees and minnows that swim upstream in the silver light of the moon. Think of a starlit night when the air is so pure you can see the vault of heaven open like a fairy tale queen cascading her shimmering hair over us and opening our hearts so that all our wishes can come true. Think of these things; breathe them into your soul like the rare perfume of a dew-covered rose that trembles on a summer morning. Think of all the fairy tales that you love and cherish. Think about castles with their moats drawn up and inside the bustle of life: the markets, the songs of the hawkers, and the brightly-coloured clothing of the people, the cacophony of jubilant sound. Think of big, handsome knights on their chargers, pennants waving, saving beautiful damsels in distress. Do you dream of these things? Do you think about them?"

"Oh yes, Señor Poet, I think of these things all the time!"

The Poet laughed. "Excellent. And now I want you to keep that magic world firmly in your mind. No! Don't open your eyes, don't even peek!" He wagged his finger at her as she giggled.

"Now, we are going re-arrange things just a little. With your eyes still closed, I want you to put on your painter's smock and pick up your paint brush. Your blank canvas is in front of you and you are going to paint the world that you see before you in your imagination — all the wonder that is in your heart, all its splendid colours and magic, and its sounds. Use your palette wildly, open your heart wide; there is only you who can see this work of art that you are creating. There is no one to tell you what your magic world should look like, because that is the province of your soul only. Have you begun; do you see this world take shape before you?"

The little girl nodded, her face screwed up with such intensity that the Poet smiled. "Take a few more minutes and then let me know when your painting is finished, and you are happy with what you have done."

As he waited for her, a slight breeze arising from the valley brought the scent of violets into the air. In the distance, from the Mirador San Nicholas, he could hear the faint cry of a gypsy violin. Looking down into the Albaycin district, he could see the bustle of life, shadows of people merging and then parting as they went about their daily lives. Then he began to see other things too. It started as a bright light that shimmered from the rooftops of the buildings and the worn cobblestone streets and as he watched, he could see it grow in intensity and take shape. Throngs of phantoms emerged from the walls of the ancient Arab sector, Moorish warriors and nobility, their jewelled scarabs twinkling in their turbans, swaths of green and magenta and indigo blue in their garb. Then he saw scholars arguing as they walked through the bazaars, weaving their way through potters and snake charmers, and delicate maidens with almond eyes and dusky skin who walked arm in arm, peeping out furtively from beneath brightly-coloured veils.

All were garlanded in their finery and moved languidly as one, as if directed in a waltz of incredible fragility, and their spirits infiltrated the homes and niches and courtyards up and down the alleyways of their former world.

Of course, the people of Granada passed through them; it was as though they did not exist. Because of their indifference, they did not notice the growing looks of despair on the faces of these phantoms as they slowly comprehended their circumstances, nor did they hear the wails that arose from their lips when they realized that they had lost a treasure of inestimable value.

The modern Granadinos ignored them completely when these phantoms raised their hands to Allah and cried out as one, "Why?"

Chapter Ten

He felt movement beside him. "Señor Poet, my painting is finished."

"Good! And is everything you dreamed of contained within this canvas? Castles and knights and beautiful princesses and genies too?"

"Oh, yes, and talking dogs and whispering trees and flowers that come alive for little children and dance with them in the sun." The little girl giggled, and added, "Oh, and there's a wizard in the upper right-hand corner. I think it's Merlin, and he's wearing a pointed star hat that glows when he smiles. He's got a big white wand in his right hand and right now he's smiling at the knights and damsels who are dancing on the village green. Maybe he put a spell on them." She giggled again.

"Wonderful!" The Poet laughed. "Now, for you to see the Arab world that was here, we're going to make a few geometric changes here and there, like Picasso would do. Do you know his work? Have your parents and teachers talked about him?"

The little girl nodded. "Oh yes, we have some of his pictures in our home and I've been to art galleries with my teachers and looked at his work there too."

"Good, because he is one of Spain's most important painters and he was Andalusian too! He was my friend. He painted a backdrop for one of my plays in the days when we wandered like minstrels into the heart and soul of Spain bringing her music and laughter.

"Now here's what we're going to do. We're going to sit at his feet and take a lesson from him. Let us deconstruct our dreams just a little. Why don't we place a little daub of blue here and a little burnt orange there, and oh yes, definitely bright, glorious yellow everywhere, and when we feel that we still have all the colours and the beauty of our imagined world but the lines are indistinct, a little blurred, perhaps, smudged, then we're going to add something new on top. Are you ready?"

Angelina nodded and closed her eyes once more.

"Good. Instead of castles, we're going to take a scene from Aladdin and his wonderful adventures as our inspiration. We're going to create with our palette the wonders of the Alhambra, its rich and multifaceted hues of red, gold, and green set against its skin of ivory bones or the Alcazar in Sevilla, with its forest of dizzying mosaics, room after room of beauty, columns and archways stretching into infinity. Or, better still: let us re-construct the Mezquita mosque in Cordoba. Its grandeur overwhelms us: arch upon arch of candy cane stripes, red and white as far as the eye can see. And vaulted ceilings buoyed by the prayers of the devout who whisper to God and call Him great. Let us keep Picasso with us; we still need him! Because these new palaces and places of worship are also full of geometric shapes and exotic designs and wonderful, unexpected surprises that may jar just us a little. We might feel a little disoriented at first like Picasso's audiences who cried out, 'Wait! What kind of world is this? I don't recognize this world! It has thrown me into confusion.' But I promise you, little one, that this new world we are painting is just as exotic and as transformational as one of Picasso's greatest paintings. Perhaps more so, because now we are going to lift this painting from our canvas and place it into Al-Andalus. We are going to carve its exotic geometry and its scent of Arabia into the hills and rivers of the Guadalquivir and the Darro and set its astounding beauty into the mountains and the sea, where it fits naturally. But wait! There's one more thing to do. To give our world life, we must breathe. Breathe, Angelina! Breathe life into this painting and cause it to come into being, like the breath of God who created us. And then let us sit back to see that what we have done is good. Ah, such beauty, don't you agree? And now, little one, let the magic begin."

Angelina laughed when she looked into her heart and her mind's eye to see the painting they had created. Then her face grew serious. "Are my castles and my knights and ladies still here, and Merlin, is he still there too?"

"Oh, yes, more so! Because all we have added on top of your painting was the exoticism of the Arab world with their viziers and Caliphs and jinn. You see, my angel, in their time, the air was suffused with the magic of genies who granted wishes and who made themselves visible to people. Sometimes they scared and tricked them too. But the division between the worlds, between heaven and earth, and hell below, was more transparent, and what we would call 'magic' now was commonplace back then. Because at that time, everything was possible, and nothing stopped the heart of the Arab people from imagining a perfect world, a world in perfect flower. Now, open your eyes and let us climb onto that magic carpet and take a closer look."

Angelina rubbed her eyes and then turned to look through her Poet's heart. She saw the towers and spires of ancient Córdoba rise before her. And now, with his hand in hers, they walked through its narrow streets, white-walled and fused with peonies and carnations that tumbled across balustrades and down balconies while muffling the sound of chatter and gossip that ran from house to house, its discourse rambling down alleyways and through courtyards at random. It was a world that teemed with bustle: horses and riders festooned with colour and jewels, heads held high with a certain hauteur that was magnificent. There were donkeys carrying wearying loads, heads lowered in patience, oblivious to the caravans of laughter and commerce and loud melodramatic bickering around them. Alive! Everything was so gloriously alive. Under the canopies of the grand souk in the centre of the city, hawkers mingled with the nobility and wove a precarious path through snake charmers and magicians. Water carriers wandered like mendicant monks through the throng as well, the bells on their turbans tinkling merrily to the silver rhythm of the cups that jangled at their waists. Delicious aromas of lamb and spices mingled with the scents of musk and frankincense while Moors, Jews, and Christians alike swirled through the marketplace in search of their daily needs. There was great abundance in evidence: star fruit from Samarkand, durians from Asia, rich tapestries from Persia, mother of pearl earrings from Damascus, and bars of gold and silver from Baghdad and Egypt.

Angelina marvelled at the wealth and colour. Why was her own world so barren? The markets that she and her Mama frequented in Granada were not like this; they were pale shadows of what she now saw before her. In her world there was no riotous sense of celebration, no sense of hospitality, just muted tones of a former greatness. Where was the communion? Where was the meeting place between friends and families? What had happened to this splendour? Where was the laughter, the scholarly discussions about the trajectory of the moon and the stars, and the importance of mathematics and geometry? Where was Maimonides, also known as Mūsā ibn Maymūn, and who now remembered his great discourses on the Torah? Were Socrates and Plato discussed with such passion? Who now remarked on how the scholars of that day sought a synthesis between the works of Aristotle and the greatest of their Arab thinkers, with vigorous debate coming from Christians, Jews, and Arabs combined? Where were the modern-day troubadours in evidence at every turn, delighting their audiences and caressing them with honeyed words full of oblique meaning? How pale and diminished was her world in comparison!

As they continued their sojourn, Angelina saw children running in and out of the market stalls and the shops, their antics lovingly condoned by the laughter of the adults who chased them away and admonished them. "Do people live here too?" she whispered.

The Poet laughed and said, "You can talk out loud, Angelina. No one can hear you; I made sure of it! Yes, many generations of families have lived in these great souks and continue to do so. It is the same throughout the Arab world now. All you need to do is travel to Morocco and into the cities of Fes and Marrakech to see these souks today. The people there carry on the traditions of their forbearers with pride. And in Morocco you can see the remnants of the swirling together of these great traditions, where the people of the Book lived together communally and with respect. In the souk in Marrakech, for instance, down an ancient alleyway that runs with wild dogs and barefoot children, impoverished and poor, there still exists an ancient Jewish 'mellah' or neighbourhood and a very old synagogue where a Rabbi pores over his Torah. This goes back to the tradition of shelter that the Arabs provided the Jews when they were dispersed from Spain during the terrible years of the Inquisition. The Kings of Morocco protected the Jews and ensured that they were able to keep their religion and traditions alive."

They stood and silently watched the melee around them. "Look at that shoemaker over there." He pointed to an old man who sat in the doorway of his shop. Clad in a flowing jellaba and a woven skull cap, his focus fused on the task at hand, patiently weaving his thread round and round an ancient sole and then spitting occasionally onto the leather to keep its shine alive.

"He will teach this trade to his sons and they will teach it to their sons and when he dies, they will inherit his shop. They will embrace his learning and his pride of workmanship and the tradition will continue. This shop has become a permanent part of their family. Protected from the prying eyes of the world, the house that is attached to this shop has witnessed generations come into life, mature, and then die. Everything has its place in this society. Here in this souk, the homes and the workplaces of these families are one. Come." He took her hand again.

There was an order to the souk that was now slowly becoming apparent to Angelina. Everything did indeed have its place and as she looked around her, she could see its patterns starting to emerge. Over there was a spice stall manned by a father and his adult sons. The old man bickered happily with his customers whilst performing a pantomime of exquisite agony in his haggling and remonstrating that left his sons, and their customers, in stitches. The spices, as an accompaniment to this perfor-mance, were piled high into mountainous heaps of saffron and rich orange-red, deep forest green, and brilliant yellow, all carefully positioned in blue and white porcelain bowls, row upon row, each a monument of artistry. Beside this was a tea shop where men sprawled on cushions next to low mosaic tables smoking their hookahs and engaging their comrades in animated conversation with great, munificent gestures. They too, wore their jellabas and on their feet were babouches of red, yellow, and indigo peeking out from beneath their robes. Next to the men were shops containing mysterious clothing for women, shoes and undergarments and gorgeous watered silks. There were rows upon rows of strange garments that Angelina was sure her mother didn't wear. She watched as the women buzzed through these items, reaching out for bright bolts of cloth and bargains, their eyes equally bright with laughter behind their veils.

Then they came to a leather workshop, and as they went inside, Angelina's attention was drawn upward through the slats that opened to the sky. She saw huge vats of dyes: reds, blues, and yellows all being tended by men and young boys who stirred the pots patiently whilst adding mysterious substances at propitious moments. She wrinkled her nose at the smell. It was harsh and acrid, and she pitied the men who worked under the merciless sun to ensure a steady supply of these dyes to the merchants below for the embellishment of their exquisite goods. The emblem of their labours, the reds, blues, and yellows that they stirred and fussed over like lovers, was also deeply embedded in their skins. The stamp of their trade flowed through their veins from an early age.

They moved silently along the alleyway and then the Poet pulled her into a warren of bright colours. Woven fabrics fell from sky to earth like a Bedouin's tent. In the shop of a wealthy rug seller, they stood and watched the merchant in animated conversation with his customers. They were seated on embroidered cushions and low chairs inlaid with mother of pearl and all around them were scattered layer upon layer of rugs and kilims that crept up the walls and fell gently back to the floor on the far side of the room: soft tapestries of pinks and blues, like a lazy summer morning, along with those that contained brilliant geometric shapes, befitting a sultan's palace. Both parties, buyers and sellers alike, were solemn in the pause before the negotiations. Exquisitely polite, meticulously sipping mint tea from delicate crystal glasses, each took the measure of the other. Then, as if long rehearsed, in response to a subtle clue genetically transmitted, perhaps a simple touch of the ear lobe, or a rub against the side of a nose to a spouse and a vague nod in reply, the buyer confidently asked, 'How much for this one?' And the pandemonium of their negotiations began.

Beside this was a madrassa and Angelina could

see little boys in a semicircle around the Imam. Each recited verses from their Koran, their tiny voices lost in the cacophony of the world around them. Beyond them stood the mosque, and she could see men, serious and intense, circling a mosaic fountain in heated discussion, pillars of exquisite geometry bracketing their movements. At the same time, she heard the bells peal high into the crystal air from a nearby church and then watched as Jewish scholars passed by with their scrolls and dark clothing, seemingly immune to the life around them, their sons walking behind, respectfully.

There was colour everywhere! The reds, purples, and gold brocade of the nobility mingled with the more modest dress of the sellers, and the sun glinted off the jewels in the turbans of the royals. She smelled the ancient musk of Arabia, its cinnabar and almonds, its cardamom and perfume, and she saw veiled and mysterious ladies walk through the throng, glorious in their diaphanous gowns, and their kohl-rimmed beauty.

Through the sounds of the throng, she heard ancient prayers being intoned to heaven. The Poet led her to a nearby hill and they looked down to see mosques next to synagogues and churches, each standing peaceably and intact.

"How many people live here?"

"At the apogee of this great city, Angelina, when

she was called the 'Jewel of the World,' there were close to 900,000 souls that walked through her heart. There were few cities of the same sophistication and grandeur in the western world at that time. The cities in Europe were much smaller, and greatly impoverished in comparison.

"Look over there," he said, as he pointed towards a man slowly walking towards them. "That is a nobleman from France, and he is here to get advice from the physicians and scientists on an ailment that he has had for years and for which he cannot find relief in his country." They watched as he walked through the gates of an unprepossessing building and into the courtyard beyond that was laden with the scent of lemon trees and hibiscus.

"Cordoba was a magnet for scholars and mathematicians and scientists from all over the world, and the poetry that sprang from the heart of this great city alone raised her in the estimation of all who sought to emulate her, but in vain. For how could you emulate the exoticism of her heart! This was a jewel in the crown of the Umayyad dynasty, and it remained so for close to three hundred years. And look, Angelina, look at the mingling of these cultures. Do you see unhappiness, tension, or racial hatred on these streets?"

The little girl looked closely at the throng below her and then shook her head.

"Precisely! That is my point. What ultimately destroyed this civilization was internal divisiveness, not the pitting of one religion against another. That came later. It has always been the bane of the Arab world that pettiness, quarrelling, and incipient tribal inclinations kept them at each other's throats in a state of perpetual divisiveness. Unity has rarely been possible. Come, there are other wonders we must explore."

She heard the trill of lutes in the gardens and saw blushing women and amorous men in a gentle dance of love while, all around them, lush and scented with pomegranates and oranges, were the famous gardens of Arabia, an oasis in the middle of a barren Christendom that crept ever closer, like a menacing predator.

The Poet sighed. "Angelina, look at this world; look at its beauty and elegance! Look at its refinement and its joy. Memorize it, for it will never be seen again, not in this way. Al-Andalus was a bright jewel in the scabbard of a scimitar, glowing and eternal, hanging in the vault of heaven for the briefest whisper of time. And then it vanished like an elusive genie, back into Aladdin's lamp."

Angelina's face was rapt as she stared at the beauty around her. Nowadays she only saw such sights in a magical movie or read about such wonders in a fairy tale. Her heart pounded with excitement.

"Come!" said the Poet. "Walk with me!"

And with that they were back in their own world once more, surrounded by the gardens of the Alhambra and the gentle sound of water shushing through fountains.

Chapter Eleven

The Poet's voice was soothing as he took Angelina by the hand, allowing her to move through the veil of time between the fabulous world they had just left to the heart of what was now the remnants of that world.

"As we look at the world around us and seek to understand our Arab predecessors, perhaps it might help if we put it in the way of a fable. Imagine the Nazrid palace that we see around us now as a living, radiant entity, full of riches and great wisdom. Inject into this world the caliphs and their queens, and the women of the caliph's harem. Imagine them walking with their children around jewelled gardens and fountains of delight. How they revered water, these desert people! Imagine them entering their exquisite abodes, precisely designed and calibrated to greet the sun and the moon in season, and perfectly aligned with the mathematical beauty of the stars. Instead of this lifeless space that we now see before us, hear the sweet songs of the women, refined and beautiful, women who were much revered as troubadours and poets. Imagine their garments, radiant! Rich and glorious fabrics, exquisite silks embraced by the amber and musk of the Arabian Desert.

"For you see, my angel, when the Arabs came into our world and ruled Iberia for all those long years, they civilized us. They saved us from the Visigoths and brought us not only the scent of the deserts and the mountains, but the very best of their learning and their culture, so much more refined than anything seen in the rest of Europe at that time. As we just saw, they left us with a legacy of mathematics, astronomy, science, medicine, and the beauty of the love poems of their troubadours. But far greater than this is the legacy of a culture of tolerance towards all people, where the Jew and the Christian were welcomed, and where they continued their own great traditions under the rule of their Arab masters.

"Such was the tolerance of these people, such was their directive that they received from their great Prophet to learn, to always learn, and never let a day pass by without learning more. Because of this, the Umayyad rulers gathered together the greatest scribes and poets and scholars from all traditions and a great flowering of ideas occurred. Ah, what an incredible time it must have been. How I wish I had lived then! No wonder Boabdil wept terribly as he was driven from this place, before darkness fell and we descended into primitivism once more. Poor, sad Spain, always so much greatness at her fingertips, always so much beauty in her verse and in her poems and in her art, and all of this would have been revered by the Arabs because they have always been known as great lovers of beauty and refinement, and hospitality. But then tragedy struck. Spain and Christendom turned on the Arabs and the Jews. They killed their dreams along with their poems and their thinkers, and they obscured their fragrance with the ashes of a repressive desolation.

"Angelina, Andalucía is a deep wound for the Arab people. When they invaded her shores, they had no intention of remaining here. They were nomads; in fact, the word 'Arab' means exactly that. As they had done in history since the time of the Prophet, they took over lands and countries, left their regents there to govern, and then moved on. They left the traditions of the Christians and the Jews intact. But here, in Andalucía, something happened. Perhaps it was the dance of the ocean in the warm breeze, perhaps it was the beauty of the Vega, maybe it was the mist hovering over the mountains or the vibrancy of the flowers, but when they came to this land they were enchanted by its magic, and they could not leave her. They put aside their nomadic ways and settled here, determined to remain."

"But, Señor Poet," the little girl looked confused, "we are taught in our school that when they came here, they hated the infidels and tried to force their pagan ways upon them. Didn't they force them to pray to their god? That's what we were told. My parents tell me this too. Didn't they try to make them hate Jesus and bow to Allah instead?"

"Hate Jesus? Angelina, no! They revered Jesus! They revered him and still do, as a great prophet and messenger. They revere his mother, our blessed Mary. Mary is mentioned in the Koran more than any other woman: fourteen times! They did not force anyone to convert. Unlike the Christian knights who decimated and murdered everyone on their 'holy' crusades and who, in the capture of Jerusalem, murdered thousands of Muslim men, women, and children wantonly in the name of the same Jesus, the Arabs respected the people of the Book and left them to worship in their own churches and synagogues. Mostly. But this was also prudent! If all of those whom they conquered had converted to Islam, then who would have supported them financially, who would have supported their towns and cities and governments? Those subjects that they subdued could keep their faith, their customs, and their places of worship, but it was upon them that the burden of taxation also fell. Were they harsh, yes! Were lives lost, absolutely! But they won this land easily. The old alliance of the Roman and

Visigoth world could not stand up to the passion of these desert people and capitulation occurred quickly. In many cases, they were welcomed. They were certainly not as barbaric as the Christians who decimated this culture in the 'Reconquista' and who, in Granada in 1492, forced Jews and Muslims to convert under the pain of torture or face the fires of the Inquisition if they did not. In the end, they were driven out of this land and sent into exile anyway, away from their cherished homeland, while a great culture was destroyed.

"Tell me, Angelina, who was more barbaric?"

Chapter Twelve

He took her hand and they walked from the Generalife over a little bridge and along a path of flowers and trees and ancient stones. The sky was azure, with wisps of clouds shaped like angel wings.

Angelina breathed in the aromas of the flowers and felt great peace move into her heart. She had not felt happiness like this for a long time. It was as though the warmth of the day and her new friend's love melted the ice that had encased her. It was one of those moments when everything felt possible, when everything was perfect. She sighed deeply and then turned to him.

"You promised to tell me about the Gitanos, Señor Poet. Why do you love them so much?"

"Ah, the gypsies!" The Poet's face lit up. "It is their songs, I think. I love their songs, Angelina; they move me to a deep place within myself, a place where few see because I do not trust the motives of many. I know people's hearts, you see." He shook his head ruefully. "They cannot hide from me.

"But the gypsy lament slips effortlessly through the filaments of my resistance; their 'cri de cœur' pierces me and reminds me of my grief too. They hold up a mirror to my soul. And just as I could not exist without creating my poems and my plays, I believe they would perish without their music and their dance. If they did not have an outlet for their passion, and for the pain of rejection they feel every day, I think they would slowly turn to stone, wide-eyed and mute; mouths opened wide in a soundless scream. Until one day they would wither away and become dust, and then leave us on the wings of the wind." The Poet sighed again.

"Angelina, to sing, to create, to write, to paint, is everything to those of us who feel most alive when we express ourselves in these ways. What would Modigliani have done without his passion? Could Van Gogh and Gauguin have created such beauty without theirs? It is the Muse that humbles us. She is our Mistress and teases us to come closer. She impels us to extract the base ore from our souls and, through an excruciating alchemy, present our vision to the world, like Prometheus did when he brought us back the light. This is not something we elect to do! We don't say 'oh, this is Sunday and I have run out of things to ponder and to do, so let us paint something!' No, it is subtler than that. We do not select Art. Art selects us. And through countless hours and days of ecstasy and sorrow, sometimes not in equal measure, we become her slave, and her apprentice. Over time we realize that we have no option but to obey her whisperings in our souls. Her will becomes ours.

"I would perish, little one, just like the gypsies, if I could not express myself through art. Why? Because of my essential loneliness, a loneliness that I have borne since earliest memory and one that was not assuaged by the camaraderie of others. Oh yes! I was the life of the party, the one who dominated all discourse and laughter. But what my friends did not know, or few did, was that behind that mask of gaiety my soul was tormented and in great pain, and it was so for most of my life. My 'duende,' my personal demon, tore my heart in two, and soon I fell in love with death. I was fascinated by her dance. Death became a character in many of my poems and plays. I dreamt of her and hence my own death, always. But on the surface of life few knew the extent of my sorrow. Perhaps God did. Perhaps not." A wave of sorrow passed over his face.

"I was always so different from others around me. I would wither at the glances of society and their disapproval when I tried to communicate my dreams, when I tried to point out how far from grace we had all fallen. They treated me like the aliens they were, so dwarfed in their grasping natures and in the blind acceptance of the status quo. And so instead, my dreams took the form of letters and verse, and all the things I wanted to say to this person or that flowed like liquid honey from my pen and formed a golden elixir on the page.

"My passion travelled through my veins effortlessly. It began in my heart, then moved through my arms and fingers and onto the page. If I could not express myself through my writing, I would have perished from loneliness. My 'duende' would finally have rebelled and overwhelmed me and I would have turned to stone too. So, it is easy for me to have affection for the gypsies because I identify with them so completely. I am just like them. I have watched and wondered about them my entire life and admired their freedom. And their kindness. I admire the freedom and strength they have to be themselves, against a scornful society and its expectations. The freedom to live with a code of their own, knowing they are despised. What strength!

"In the Vega where I was raised, I found my home with them. They always made me feel welcome. They saw this slightly melancholic boy, a little sickly, who preferred to listen to the wind as it carried their songs aloft rather than spending time with his friends. I was nurtured on their music and sat close to their breast and drank in their poetry.

"When I grew older, I would wander into their barrios and sit in my favourite café or bar. Many times, I was the only non-Gitano there. But they knew me and acknowledged me. I would watch them with a deceptive casualness. The evenings began as one would expect in any bar or café in Madrid or Barcelona. There was much laughter and conviviality and over time the thrum of conversation grew in intensity.

"Then spontaneously, without any prior indication that this was going to happen, almost as if a cord had been drawn between a singer and the Almighty, a sigh would leave a certain man's lips, like vapour. The room hears this and all conversation ceases. Another sigh follows. Then this sigh turns into a low moan followed by a wail, and others from his clan, no matter where they are in the room, come over as if drawn by a magnetism that they cannot ignore. They surround this man and start to clap rhythmically, slowly, methodically, and with great assurance. One man picks up a guitar, and another an overturned milk crate which he then starts to tap gently. Together they join this man whose wails have now filled the room with electric pathos. The musicians watch him closely. They commiserate with him when a certain pitch of feeling emanates from his heart, and this encourages the singer to go further.

"And then, as though by a mysterious inner signal, another man walks onto the stage and finds that his hands and arms have started to move involuntarily like a new butterfly in summer experiencing the ecstasy of release. They weave around his head in the ancient dance of centuries, and softly his passion grows too. It is as though his limbs become a bellows that invites the fire to leap and the warmth to spread throughout the room. The movements of the dancer become more dramatic. His feet stomp out his emotion precisely and his face, always in pain, bears the full expression of his birth. From within the mists of this drama a Señorita emerges and silently joins her partner. They weave their bodies together like ancient serpents cast out of paradise and suddenly you realize that you, and everyone else in the room that is not privy to the secret of their song, are utterly irrelevant. A wall of mist separates the uninitiated from them, and they are always surprised to see us after the last wail leaves the singer's lips and the dancers pant in exhaustion, their trance broken. The claps and the cheers do not move them. They shrug and move away indifferently. But with the last sigh the air shifts, the magic they created leaves the room, and the world becomes ordinary again. People pick up their glasses and conversations resume. The gypsies are forgotten completely.

"When I talk to them about their songs, they say this is the moment where they find God. This act of gnosis allows them to connect with the Divine inside themselves because it is only through this lament that they can pierce the veil of sadness and move into a realm of ecstasy. It is their way of banishing the demons or perhaps acknowledging their existence and then exorcising them with a sigh. But to witness this you must go into barrios like Triana in Sevilla where the heart of this lament really began, and not into the mockery of the stage that passes as flamenco today."

"But I don't understand, Señor Poet, if they are as you say they are, and I believe you, then why are people so afraid of them? Why do they hate them and call them thieves and beggars and cross themselves whenever they appear?"

Angelina admitted that she was a little afraid of the gypsies herself. Their passion for life, their hauteur, was raw and filled with edges. It was not something that existed in the polite society where Angelina had been raised. It was as if they knew no boundaries, or if they did, they walked through them, contemptuously.

"Angelina, please understand me!" The Poet's voice rose in passion. "There are some gypsies who are bad and perpetuate the stigma of the beggar and the thief. But there are those in our own 'society' who do the same and more, and yet we don't seem to vilify them quite as much. I have always believed that the way you look at the world reflects your soul, and how you feel about yourself."

They sat in silence. Angelina certainly felt this statement to be true and she wondered then at the perspectives she had been raised with, the constant and persistent one-dimensional focus of Catholicism, for instance. Did the indoctrination she had received at home, in school, and at church leave her with any independent thought? Where did those teachings end, and her own independent reflections begin? Could she separate the two? She also thought about the dire teachings themselves, hellfire and damnation, the 'Original Sin' that she and other children had been born with, and she wondered if, in the face of these unremitting teachings, a gypsy heart like hers even stood a chance? No wonder she was always in so much trouble!

Her earliest memories consisted of thinking there was something wrong in the world somehow. She was frustrated to find a name for this feeling, but she knew it was there. There was something wrong with the way society told them to live, a society in which the church still held a such powerful position here in Spain. She frequently felt as though she didn't belong in this world somehow, that her world existed beyond the veil, in another realm altogether. She understood the Poet when he said the same thing. Her heart always sought places where she could be wild and free, where she could be herself.

The Poet broke the silence. "Do you see that flower over there?"

She nodded.

"What do you see?"

"I see a beautiful red fairy dancing in the sun. She is happy! What do you see?"

The Poet smiled. "I see a lovely woman in red, with radiant and piercing beauty, dancing seductively to entrance her lover. But that is my point: this is the same flower, and yet we look at it differently. Everyone will see that flower through the refracted prism of their own lens, a lens that reflects their history, cultural conditioning, thoughts, anxieties, or passions. No one will see that flower in the same way. Unlike us they may look at her and say 'oh, what a nuisance, look at that annoying red weed, just another poppy in my garden' and so on. Others will see her as a form of drug to harvest so that her overall beauty is ignored in anticipation of the hallucinatory beauty they will experience later.

"So it is with the way we look at people, or a people. Every expert of the human soul will tell you that those who look at gypsies with scorn feel scorn for themselves; those who deprecate their freedom feel trapped in their own existence and feel quite 'unfree.' Gypsies defy the norm! They do not bow to our laws; they have the audacity to be free. They have the audacity to traverse all boundaries that entrap the soul. They wander as their spirits call them, and their siren song is their only guiding star. They take their homes and their few possessions with them when they go. They are not bound by the conventions that enslave us, and which have rendered us impoverished in comparison. But then, what is poverty and what is wealth? To the gypsies, we are the impoverished ones. We are the ones who are so enslaved to the material world that we squander our precious lives in search of fool's gold and are never satisfied. That pot of gold at the end of the rainbow is always around the next corner, in the next position that we hold, in the next lover that falls into our arms, in the next poem that we write, and all the while the sluggish, endless pain inside us grows, not drowned at all by the way we try to fool ourselves with our temporary euphoria. And then, one day our souls finally groan in agony, and wither away."

The Poet shook his head ruefully. "Angelina, in many ways the gypsies are a threat. Why? Because they threaten the fragile code of life in which we have enveloped ourselves and which we have pronounced sacrosanct. They feed our egos so that we start to feel more superior, beyond reproach, because after all, our view of life is supported by the larger society, even though that may be a false view of life based upon a society that is flawed! Reality is relative, after all. It is a short step from there to take refuge in a society of similar souls and collectively view those on the periphery as the 'Other.' The trouble is, Angelina, in our society, in this confusing amalgam of cultures that we have come to call 'Spain,' there are many on the periphery. And once the 'Other' is identified in this way it becomes easy to denigrate them, and then to eradicate them. 'Pah!' you say, 'look at these vermin, these people who dare to live outside the borders of our world. They are a disgrace! Let us destroy them.' And so, they do.

"But what the persecutors fail to realize is that our soul is the provenance of God alone and can never be destroyed. The gypsies know this, and it is this knowledge that lies at the heart of their treasure; indeed, this is the treasure of all those who face persecution. This is the one area of our existence where those who persecute us can never touch. Your soul is your temple, Angelina! The world of tyrants cannot touch the purity within you, the passion and the dreams. Not unless you give them permission to do so. The tyrants belong to the external world only; that is where their 'god' lives. But they are internally weak and rely on this external bullying as compensation. We have seen the full brutality of this in Spain. The tyrants think that they can capture and destroy the body and by doing so, they believe they have destroyed our essence and removed us from existence. But that is not so! 'Evil' has no soul. It can only discern that which the ego feels are in its self-interest and nothing deeper. It is utterly empty and banal and thinks it can destroy wantonly. But it thinks this way because it does not know the Muse, the Divine, and the Transcendent that lies within us all. It even lies within those who commit evil, although they have forgotten this. THAT is who we are; the body is an encasement for our souls only.

"The gypsies know that no matter their external circumstances, their truth and their passion can be accessed very easily. By joining with their kinsmen and singing the songs that have been passed down from one generation to another, they are keeping their ancestral spirit alive, and with it, their souls. When I hear them sing, I hear myself sing also."

"Do you feel their pain too?" Angelina felt certain that she did.

"Yes, little one, their pain is also mine. Their 'duende' is the demon I have tried to expel from my soul all my life."

"But you were not shunned like they are; how can you know the pain of being a gypsy?"

"But I do know this pain! I know the pain of being ostracized. I dared to live my life authentically, in full freedom. I know this pain; I experienced it every day. I saw the condescension of those who were embedded in a world of values I did not respect. They looked at me with eyes glutted by materialism and ambition and I knew they despised me. And in those moments, my 'duende' raised its ugly head and told me that I would never fit into their world no matter how hard I tried, and for the briefest of moments I was filled with great pain.

"But then I reached inside to gather my strength, like the gypsies. I knew that there was no other recourse for me if I were to survive. And I also surrounded myself with people who were just like me. We became our own community and then I looked at these people and thought, 'Yes, the world honours you because you are of the world and I am not. You will always be in your own time. But you do not have my riches. You do not have what I have, and your caprice and greed will always prevent you from knowing what I know. You do not have Romance, Love, and Mystery in your souls. Why? Because your god demanded that you exorcise them in order to be subservient to him.' They say, 'Give me your soul and I will give you material riches beyond your wildest dreams!' Fool's gold. But I say unto them, 'Where your eyes are opaque, mine are alive. Where your heart has died, mine is bursting with the songs of the Vega, the breath of the flowers, and the scent of the moon. Where you are enslaved by your materialism and your need to have more, I am free to pursue the richness of my soul.' And in those moments, I knew that I was wealthy indeed."

Chapter Thirteen

"I don't understand one thing, Señor Poet. Why would they hate you for being on the side of the people, for caring about them? Isn't that what the church tells us Christ did too?"

"The church?" The Poet laughed incredulously. "Yes, the church did indeed tell us that, and I believed them. There was no one more devout than I. My friends used to laugh at me when I left them early on a Saturday night in Madrid to go home so that I could be up early for Mass the next day. I used to love the ancient scent of sanctity wafting over my mind and senses when I was in prayer. My soul soared with the purity of the sacred music and I wept inside for my love of God. I loved the rituals and the pomp, the solemn wonder of the sacristy and the host. I was the first into church in the morning, prostrate before the Virgin.

"But, Angelina, our mother church also hid armaments behind the veil of the Madonna for later use by the fascists. The cardinals and the bishops held the cross in one hand and rifles in the other. Evil lurked behind the sign of absolution. Oh no, not directly! But their complicity doomed them. Fascism and Catholicism are one. The fascists hid their arms in the convents and monasteries too, beneath the skirts of benevolence and compassion. Not in all cases, because there were many of the clergy who rebelled against this evil and who suffered as innocents at the hands of the Republicans. The church was afraid of what they called 'liberalism.' To them any progressive thought that strayed from their beliefs was like a cancer that needed to be uprooted. They railed against any reforms that the Republicans wanted to introduce that would cause the people to think for themselves. They especially balked against proposed changes in the schools that hinted at religious study being removed from its place of prominence. 'Oh no!' they said. 'We cannot have this! Because it would dilute our power over the masses and their unformed minds.' The church!" The Poet shook his head sadly.

"Listen, Angelina, although you are living in a time that is modern and you are immersed in a contemporary world that thinks more progressively, when I was young things were much different. All the liberties and the way of life you take for granted now were earned on the backs of those who struggled for those liberties and often paid with their lives. I surrounded myself with friends who were filled with ideas of change and progress. We were restless for the old ways to fall. Yes, some would call this 'revolutionary,' even 'anarchical.' It was a revolution against the bourgeoisie and the landowners and a railing against the church and its doppelganger, the government. For me as well, it was a revolution against the government's henchmen, the Guardia Civil, who were their anvil.

"All I wanted was freedom, Angelina! Freedom like the gypsies. Freedom to live the way I wanted to live and with whom, freedom to rid my life of the stifling traditions that screamed 'conformity.' Freedom from 'pious morality' which hypocritically accompanied these traditions, and which formed the backbone of the elite and the status quo. Freedom to be who I am, in every sense of the word. And for this I was an enemy of the Nationalists, and a dangerous one."

"But I don't understand, Señor Poet, why would the government have hated you so much? They could not have known you the way I do, your kindness and love and your gentleness." She reached over and touched his cheek gently.

"They could not have seen your smile or felt your love of life. Or the way that you are like a little child sometimes. No one who looks at a flower the way you do or sees angels in the clouds and moonbeams in a child's hair can possibly be hateful. What did you do to them that caused them to hate you?"

He shook his head ruefully. "Angelina, I have mentioned this term to you once before. Do you know what it is to be a 'Red?'"

"Oh yes, Senor! It is a term that even today my parents say in soft voices, almost in whispers, as though the walls of our home would mouth our conspiracy back to the government. They said that in the olden days when the war broke out the Reds tried to destroy our country by introducing a great evil through their words and beliefs."

"Evil? Destroy our country?" The Poet shook his head sadly. "No, Angelina, it was not the 'Reds' or Communism that destroyed this country; fascism and the church did that, along with ancient wounds that stood as a barrier amongst the people and caused them to turn against their neighbours and even those within their families. The Nationalists tried to paint the 'Reds' as the devil when really the only devil that stalked this land was hatred inside the human heart, on both sides. Certain unscrupulous people used the excuse of the war to wage vendettas against their enemies and to get even with those who had harmed them."

"Then why did they hate the 'Reds' so much? Why are they still so afraid of them?"

"Angelina, at one time it would be have been rare

to find a student or intellectual in this country, and indeed throughout Europe and North America, who was not affected by Communism and by the philosophy of Karl Marx. How could you not be? Whether you hated the communists or not, what they stood for in the purest sense was liberation. The philosophy of communism, its original intent, was one that stood for caring. It stood for liberation and equality in a world of gross inequities: the poor and the enslaved, the serfs and peasants on the one hand, feeding the maw of the beast, the capitalists, the landowners and the bourgeoisie on the other. The aristocracy did not view the serfs as human; they were slaves who turned the wheel of their own prosperity, nothing more.

"When I was young, there was terrible poverty and injustice in this country, in most countries. There still is! You cannot escape its reach. A walk through the streets of New York, Havana, Barcelona or Madrid at that time should have stirred the conscience of a beast. Terrible! The society that we had in Spain and in Europe, its inherent unjust structure, was built on a caste system, with the elite at the top and all others below them, feeding their entitlement. There was no crossover allowed. Once you were born into your station, nothing could free you. The pompous certitude of the elite was a poison running through the veins of the impoverished who worked slavishly to meet their needs, and who were treated like detritus in return. Communism tried to address these inequities. For me, it was marvellous to read *The Communist Manifesto*, it was liberating to know that a great visionary had risen above class differences, heard the howling rage of the oppressed, and then put pen to paper to confront it. For those of us who were students at this time, and yes, most of us who lived at La Residencia in Madrid were of the privileged class, la 'crème de la crème' and the future leaders of Spain, this thought, this notion, this way of thumbing our noses at the 'elite' was intoxicating, and some of us, those with a conscience and a weariness, a deadly weariness of the status quo, embraced the philosophy completely. How could you not? How could you turn your back on the terrible inequities and suffering of the people? You would be a monster if you did.

"Angelina, they killed me for many things. They killed me for my words, for the power of my poems, and for my prose. For the way I put their atrocities towards the gypsies under a microscope, for the way I named the Guardia Civil as their murderers. Never underestimate the power of the word! It moves and dismantles nations; it re-arranges the landscape of the human and the political heart. A poet, a writer, and a philosopher have great power, far more than ten thousand guns. Never forget that, Angelina. That is the greatest lesson of all."

Chapter Fourteen

The Poet sat quietly, and Angelina watched his face closely as sadness replaced the anger that was stamped there. She reached over and took his hand and waited for him to speak again. She sensed his "duende" now. It moved up from his soul and found expression in his eyes. She knew and loved him well enough to sit silently and wait.

"I was in love when they killed me," he said softly. "I was in love with a beautiful man and it was so sad because after all my years of anxiety about my inclinations and who I am inside, this radiant being came into my life just as I left it. I wept most of all because I knew when they drove us away on that dark morning, as I sat in the back of the truck with two other 'anarchists' who framed me like Christ's thieves, that I would never see him again. I would never touch his beautiful face and tell him how much I loved him and how much his touch had healed me and dried my tears. I had never known love like this before; I did not know it could exist in such perfect form!

His tenderness and absolute adoration were like a holy salve on my scarred and tortured soul, pulling me back from an abyss that constantly beckoned. I thought I would forever remain unloved and misunderstood! But without words, he waved his hands over my body and soul. Kissing me gently on the lips, he brought me back to life. I never had a chance to tell him any of this."

Tears slid down his cheeks and Angelina reached out to dry them gently with the sleeve of her dress. "I wrote some of my purest love songs for him; I gave him some of my best poetry and begged him not to share this with others as it was a sacred talisman of our love. And when I left him behind in Madrid that fateful July morning as I returned to Granada, I thought that it would only be moments, a brief ephemeral sigh, before we would see each other again........"

The Poet stopped as his tears engulfed him, and Angelina said softly, "There, there," and she kept a tight hold on his hand until they subsided.

"Worst of all, I think I was killed because of this. I suspect that, along with the perceived anarchy of my poems and plays, I was also executed because of my personal preferences and the way I defined myself as a man. And the absolute way I insisted on living my life in full freedom, knowing who I was."

Angelina looked at him questioningly. "What do you mean, Señor Poet?"

The Poet looked at her and sighed deeply. "Angelina, sometimes there are people in the world who know, they know from an early age that they do not fit in. They do not fit into their society or into the preconceived role that society has laid out for them. As they grow and look around them, they know deep inside that they are not thinking the same thoughts as others, they do not view the world in the same way, they do not even view a blade of grass on a summer morning in the same light. Where one sees brown arid wasteland, another sees rich veins of purple and indigo waving in the mists of a fairyland. The Vega in her loveliness has a sheen and an intensity that is felt by these people, as though the spirits of the Earth rise to counsel them upon birth and never allow the veils to descend over their eyes and obscure their vision. This is the 'sight' of visionaries and artists that we have spoken about. This is how painters like Picasso viewed their world, and certainly Salvador Dali, my very great friend, did as well. This is how Luis Buñuel wrote about the world. They saw beyond the sheen of artifice; they saw the hypocrisy and the injustice as much as I did. For Dali, he expressed this insight brilliantly in his art, in his surrealism, while Buñuel built it into his plays and his films like *L'Age D'Or*. None of us were deceived.

"To the ones who see differently, who are different, the light shines in a rare way on everything and everyone around them. They try to fit in at first, especially when they are young, but over time they realize that they are doing their souls an injury, they are distorting who they really are, and so, if they are honest with themselves, they allow the false self, the one that society demands but doesn't sit well within them, to slip into vapour and then drift away completely.

"Angelina, I was that child, and I knew from a very early age that I was not like other children around me. Of course, my family loved me, and I adored them! I could do no wrong. They encouraged this artistic sensibility in me and marvelled when at a young age I stood up one day and recited poetry as though these words, embedded in my heart for an eternity, suddenly chose this random moment to take flight. My parents nurtured me tenderly and gave me the foundation I needed to become the poet and the playwright that I am.

"I met many at La Residencia, our school in Madrid, including Salvador Dali and Luis Buñuel who also felt that they had been 'set apart' to pursue their unique vision of the world. To refract it through the prism of their unique imaginations.

How we dreamt and laughed in those days, when everything seemed possible!

"But I am referring to more than this. Because, from the tender age of adolescence I also knew that I would never be able to fulfill my role as a husband or lover, to a woman at least. I knew that my preferences lay with men and I fought this for so long, berating myself, almost flagellating myself as we hear of monks doing to expiate their sins. I fought my demons night and day; I tried to exorcise them! But then one day I just accepted the fact that I could not change the essence of who I am because this was how God created me to be. And that was the greatest day of my life, the day when I accepted with relief, the full freedom to be who I am.

"Before I reached this stage of enlightenment, I tortured myself, Angelina, for such a long time. But I knew in my heart that I could not be happy in a 'traditional relationship' with a member of the opposite sex. Some people have the same awareness, but they push it aside and try to be 'normal' to please their parents and of course, the church. But it is impossible. They are tortured with thoughts of hell and damnation fed by the endless vitriol of the Catholic Church who hates them and calls them deviants. And so, they struggle to 'fit in' to a society that has set the standards for 'normalcy,' whatever that means, but ultimately, they know that it goes against their own nature to be someone they are not. Sometimes they can only be freest and happiest when they are with somebody who is like them, with someone of their own sex. Does this make sense to you?"

"Of course it makes sense, Señor! You are talking about being gay."

"Gay? How can these people be gay when they know the world hates them? How can they be remotely happy at all? Aren't they wretched inside that they cannot be 'normal' as their other friends are, and just be happy with a member of the opposite sex too? Do they not writhe in their beds in torment and guilt dreaming of that boy that dove into the river and swam with them on that hot summer day, instead of Marcella, his pretty sister, who picked flowers and watched them from the bank? How can there be any gaiety at all knowing that you are evil like the church says for having these thoughts?"

"No, Señor Poet, you do not understand! To be 'gay' is to be with someone who is like you, a man with a man, a girl with a girl. There are many gay people in Spain now, so we don't think about it all that much. It's no big deal."

"No 'big deal?' You talk of this as though it were nothing to you!"

"It is nothing to me, Señor, because it is accepted

and normal that some people are gay. Why would this be a 'big deal?'"

The Poet shook his head. "It appears that I blundered into my time too soon! Although I am happy for those who do not have to face this persecution now, I was born into an earlier Spain where being, how you say, 'gay,' was a very big deal. It meant that you were hated and feared in this machismo world, and sometimes even ridiculed by your closest friends. This was a torture to me, because I knew from an early age that I could not make love to a woman, although I tried!"

He ran his hand ruefully through his hair. "Angelina, when they shot me, they filled my bowels with lead and laughed that they had killed a 'pouf,' for that is what we were called. And then they went back to the bars of Granada and celebrated my death with their friends while I writhed in an unmarked mass grave, dust filling my mouth and obliterating my heart.

"They think they have escaped the blame for this crime, but I follow my murderers everywhere. I am with them when they sleep and when they play with their children. I am with them when they make love to their wives and when they try to wash away the memory of my blood from their hands. I see some them when they, too, prefer to look at young men in the baths of the hammam and then, full of hypocrisy, return home to their loveless marriages and their mock piety. I am with them in the confessional as they pour out their sins to a clergy who were also complicit in my murder through their silence even when my father, well-respected here in Granada, pleaded with them to intervene. The Archbishop of Granada alone could have saved me.

"Who did they think they were hiding from? Did they think for one moment that when they bowed in reverence before Our Lady on Sunday, portentously humble and devout, that their hearts were not seen? I watched them, these 'pious' men, from the porticos of the cathedral; I hovered over them like an angel with broken wings, my eyes weeping and my heart full of glass. I watched them set their faces in a righteous stance and mouth the prayers they had memorized since childhood, but which did not touch them, and then I watched these prayers drift away like wraiths into the cold reality of a Granada morning. I watched them waving away their evil as they left the church, smiling and shaking hands with the priest who has absolved them so that they could continue to kill and wound for another week at least. And then I was left in an empty church, the last echoes of their footsteps leaving me bereft and prostrate at the feet of my Lady.

"Beware of those with much piety, Angelina! If they say they love God and yet vengeance spews from their lips against those whom they feel God has shunned, investigate their souls instead. I do. Because no amount of praying and absolution will wash away the darkness of their deeds and the blackness of their hatred.

"I will be with these men until they die. And then, when they cross over to be where I am now, as some of them have, they will meet me there and know the terrible truth of what they have done and how their deeds have been known to God all along. And I will look at them in those moments and sadly ask, 'Why? Why did you hate me enough to kill me? Did we not grow up together? Did we not laugh and play together; did you not read my poems and encourage me? What happened to your souls that you could have allowed hatred and evil to enter so effortlessly?'"

With this the Poet grew silent and looked out at the dying of the day. Angelina followed his gaze and noticed how the sinking sun had left a varnish of gold on the underside of the trees. She watched as the gold faded slowly and felt mournful at its loss. Finally, the birds became silent, and the growing night fell over their shoulders in mute sobriety.

She turned back to him. "And then will you forgive them?"

They sat and looked at each other until the night threatened to envelop them completely.

Chapter Fifteen

The world was silent as they walked back into Granada and crossed the bridge over the River Darro. The Poet stopped and knelt so that he could look into Angelina's eyes directly.

"It is time for you to go home, Angelina. You must go back to your Mama now. She loves you."

Angelina started to protest but he put a finger over her lips.

"I know the grieving of a mother when her child disappears and never returns. On countless nights I have circled my own mother and heard her cries and felt her deep sorrow. It matched my own! I could not reach her through the veil. She could not see me like you can. Her grief was immense and I would fall down on my knees and cry with her. Sobbing, I would walk the halls of our home with her endlessly knowing that I would never feel her arms around me again. There is no pain that could possibly describe the remorse of the soul that reaches out in love but can never feel it returned. Don't do this to your Mama, Angelina. She has already lost Cristina; don't let her lose you too."

"But if I go back, I will never see you again. You're going to leave me!"

"No, Angelina, I will never leave you. You have been my angel, and now I will be yours. Every time you miss me, look into the stars on a warm Granada night for I will be there watching over you. You will see my face clearly. We are bound together now and not even God can separate us. Our love will always bind us because we both know that love is all that matters. That, and forgiveness."

He smiled ruefully at her. "You taught me that."

He kissed her cheek softly. "Now go, your Mama needs you, and give her this message from me." He reached down and whispered into her ear.

Chapter Sixteen

A ngelina ran home, her legs pumping furiously as she ran past Sacramonte and the raucous sounds of gypsy laughter. She willed herself to run faster, upward, upward, faster and faster as she flew through the serpentine streets of the ancient Arab quarter. When she finally entered her Casa she heard her mother weeping.

"Mama!" she cried.

The crying stopped and her mother ran out of the living room. Shock and then relief were evident on her face.

"Oh my God, Angelina, where have you been?"

They moved towards each other and embraced, both crying now.

"Mama," said Angelina between her hiccupping sobs, "I am sorry, please forgive me!"

"No, it is I that must apologize to you. I love you so much, Angelina! Never, never think otherwise."

Angelina stirred in her arms as their tears subsided. "I did not kill Cristina, Mama" she said fiercely, "I would never kill my sister and my best friend. I could not control that wave. I did not ask that wave to take her away."

"I know, I know," her mother started to weep again, "my heart has been so broken by her death that I forgot about my other girl who was grieving just as much. Please forgive me!"

Angelina looked up at her and pulled her mother down so that she sat in front of her. She reached up and dried her mother's eyes with the sleeve of her dress.

"There, there, don't cry Mama. I do forgive you. I did not mean to frighten you today. When I ran away, I spent the day with my friend, the Poet. I wanted to tell you about him before, but you wouldn't let me. I just left him by the River Darro. He is wonderful and I love him very much. He told me many things, and we shared many fables together. He asked me to come back to you and never let you go. He also told me to say this to you."

She leaned over and whispered into her ear and her mother heard words like "beautiful gypsy," "wild and radiant heart," and "dancing with ecstasy in the light of the moon." Her mother started to smile and then to laugh. She pulled Angelina closer, until they were completely fused as one.

Epilogue

The Poet stood and faced them quietly. He watched as his executioners pushed the others roughly into line beside him. He examined his killers closely. They were shuffling and afraid and many of them would not look in his direction, even though they had loved him once.

He still didn't understand why these men could hate him so deeply. He wondered what mechanism in their hearts could have turned them from the loving comrades they once were to the snarling, savage beasts he saw before him. Which god gave them absolution now?

Their rifles were cocked and ready, and the commander lifted his arm.

He looked skyward. The sun flickered gold and pink on the summit of the mountains as though a parallel world lived there, oblivious to the cruelty of men. Now wanting to be part of that world, he stretched up his arms to meet its embrace. He thought of his family with great love and prayed that they may always be at peace. He thought of Angelina at home, nestled in her Mama's arms, and he smiled tenderly.

Then he followed the trajectory of a skylark as she lifted herself beyond the drab, grey earth above the battlements of the Alhambra. He watched as she spiralled slowly upwards to merge with the glorious palate of colours that now radiated through the mountains.

He reached up to touch her wings. There was a clap of thunder and then they both disappeared, completely.

Gacela of the Dark Death

By Federico Garcia Lorca, 1898 – 1936, and translated by Robert Bly

I want to sleep the sleep of the apples,
I want to get far away from the busyness of the
cemeteries.
I want to sleep the sleep of that child
Who longed to cut his heart open far out to sea.

I don't want them to tell me again how the corpse
keeps all its blood,
How the decaying mouth goes on begging for water.
I'd rather not hear about the torture session the
grass arranges for
Nor about how the moon does all its work before
dawn
With its snakelike nose.

I want to sleep for half a second,
A second, a minute, a century.
But I want everyone to know that I am still alive,

That I have a golden manger inside my lips,
That I am the little friend of the west wind,
That I am the elephantine shadow of my own tears.

When it's dawn just throw some sort of cloth over me
Because I know Dawn will toss fistfuls of ants at me,
And pour a little hard water over my shoes
So that the scorpion claws of dawn will slip off.

Because I want to sleep the sleep of the apples
And learn a mournful song that will clean all the
earth away from me.
Because I want to live with that shadowy child
Who longed to cut his heart open far out to sea.

Acknowledgements

My parents gave me a great love of literature at an early age, and to their memory I give a heartfelt thanks. As a child I was lost in tales from exotic lands. Recalling some of them here came easily to me. I combine this recollection with my great love of history tempered with my strong commitment to social justice overall.

I also thank my former employer, **Metasoft Systems Inc.**, for freeing me to work in Granada, Spain, so that I could research the nooks and alleyways of Andalucía in search of Federico, who I had unashamedly fallen in love with.

In addition, I thank Tim Lindsay, CEO of **Tellwell Publishing Inc.**; my associate Caitlin Ing, Project Manager; my editor, Jen MacBride; and my designer Von Langoyan; for providing me with the vehicle to see my dreams through to completion.

And always Mikhail, my heart and my inspiration.